THE LAST WAR

RYAN SCHOW

River City Publishing

COPYRIGHT

THE LAST WAR

Cover Design by Milo at Deranged Doctor Design

Visit the Author's Website: www.RyanSchow.com

ALSO BY RYAN SCHOW

THE AGE OF EMBERS SERIES (*ONGOING*):

THE AGE OF EMBERS

THE AGE OF HYSTERIA

THE AGE OF REPRISAL

THE COMPLETE LAST WAR SERIES:

THE LAST WAR

THE ZERO HOUR

THE OPHIDIAN HORDE

THE INFERNAL REGIONS

THE KILLING FIELDS

THE BARBAROUS ROAD

THE TERMINAL RUN

THE COMPLETE SWANN SERIES:

VANNIE (PREQUEL)

SWANN

MONARCH

CLONE

MASOCHIST

WEAPON

RAVEN

ABOMINATION

ENIGMA

CRUCIFIED

FOREWORD

I was never a Pinterest person, but my wife is and she was on it enough for me to grow curious. When I got my own page, I found a crazy amount of inspiration for both the stories and the characters within them. I never wanted to keep this to myself, so I started a Pinterest board for every book in this series. These inspirational pictures include character photos, the cars and the places where my characters reside. If you're signed up for Pinterest (which is easy and free!) then visit me at: **https://www.pinterest.com/ryanschowwriter/boards/**. Also, if you haven't joined The Last War's Private Facebook Group, please click over there now as I love to chat with readers regularly as well as post cool inspirational pictures, some of the real life stories that inspired this series, cover reveals for the new books and sample chapters of books before they come out. You can request to join this private group by typing THE LAST WAR FAN GROUP in the Facebook browser (search bar). I'll see you there!

CHAPTER ONE

Forget who you were. What you did for a living. That fancy title on your business cards. Forget your paycheck, your overpriced car, the upscale neighborhood you lived in because there's no such thing as upscale anymore. Or society. Or even civility for that matter.

Oh, and if you're looking for a sense of community? Honestly, don't hold your breath. This is San Francisco, 2019.

Welcome to hell.

To survive in this post-apocalyptic cesspool, you have to un-know yourself. You have to strip away that which makes you human: your empathy, your enormous heart, all the ways you used to be and feel so special. How things are now—the big cities being stamped into ruin, relentless bombing runs, the onset of hunger and the spike in crime—you need to understand your life in this city is a death sentence.

The circumstances being what they are, doing unforgivable things, unspeakable things, is the norm. It's what you do to stay breathing. Not to belabor the point, but if you don't subscribe to the philosophy that *if you're weak, you're a corpse,* then honest to God, the window between right now and your demise is probably already closed, you just don't know it yet.

My husband, Stanton, recently told our fifteen year old daughter, Macy, "If someone's in your face and you don't feel right about them, if something feels off, just shoot them. Don't even think about it. Just do it."

Two weeks ago this would have been the most irrational statement in the world, but the way Stanton says it, you can almost believe that *he* believes he sounds completely rational. To think he was once the voice of reason in our little family of three...

Oh and me? I'm an ER nurse. Well I was, past tense. My name is Cincinnati McNamara and I spent my career at Saint Francis Memorial Hospital. I used to save lives, not take them, so hearing my husband so brazenly speak of murder is a pretty big pill for me to swallow.

We've killed though. We didn't mean to and we certainly didn't want to, but if we weren't wanting or trying to kill people and we did so anyway, what does that say about the times?

It says plenty.

Speaking of matters of life and death, before the collapse, *every* life had value. Even the junkies, the criminals and the homeless. Now the only lives with any value are mine, Stanton's, my daughter Macy's and my younger brother Rex's. I don't like thinking like this, but we really are in a survival-of-the-fittest type of world here.

I suppose we could lament our situation, this sour turn of events, but we try not to. We can't afford the mental breakdown. Even though it's coming. We tell ourselves we're not those kinds of people, the kind who just lay down and die when things get tough. We tell ourselves we're survivors, fighters.

Perhaps this is true. It could be a lie.

Either way, we are our own cheerleaders as we slog through what will surely become some urban wasteland if someone doesn't stop the brutal war being waged on mankind. Can it even be stopped? Are we the ones to do it?

Probably not.

So we navigate the streets of San Francisco, squatting where we can, eating what's available, and we try not to comprehend this city's monumental fall from grace. Instead, we dig our heels in as we grapple the impossible odds and grind against the gears of our sometimes frail and overworked minds. We do this while hiding from enemies who have taken to the streets and who kill from the air, and we do our best to ignore the voices in our heads telling us to go ahead and give up, just quit, end it once and for all and just eat that bullet.

You may be wondering, why press on when things seem so dismal? I've asked myself that same question a hundred times now. Maybe more. I have an answer, but it's flimsy, propped up on faith and desperation alone. We're praying that when the smoke clears and all the bodies have been stacked and properly burned, there will be something left to hang on to, some semblance of hope for a new life, a new future, a brand new world.

If you could see what I see, how this city turned upside down in a single afternoon, how devastation has now spread to every corner before me, perhaps you'd understand these things I'm telling you. Perhaps you'd know what I mean when I say *faith and desperation.*

But I'm getting ahead of myself. Putting the cart before the horse if you will.

Let me start at the beginning...

CHAPTER TWO

Four twelves in the ER and no one died. Hallelujah. The work week is officially over and I'm Jonesing for ten hours of uninterrupted sleep. To my SUV, I say, "Beethoven's *Symphony Number 9*." It's perfect music for almost going home. Almost. From near silence to sound, one of Beethoven's most energizing symphonies begins.

Did I tell you I'm exhausted?

Yeah, I'm depleted.

Everyone at work was like, "What are you going to do on your three days, Cincinnati?" and I was like, "Sleep, sleep, and then sleep."

First, however, I need groceries. Specifically coffee. Not for now, but for later, when I try to wake up.

Macy—our fifteen year old—she's taken to telling her friends her mother is a zombie. I have to be honest here, forty-eight hours in the ER is like sixty or seventy hours working a regular job, so yep, I absolutely feel like a zombie.

I feel like the entire cast of *The Walking Dead*.

It's noon, Macy's still in school, Stanton is halfway through work, maybe more. And me? It's all about shopping, sleeping, cooking. Yawning deep, trudging through another afternoon in the slurry of San Francisco traffic, I creep up Bush Street looking for a place to park. Twice I pass the Market Mayflower & Deli (my destination!) and twice I fail to find a spot (C'mon already!).

This is why I put on Beethoven.

To renew me.

The symphony is getting into my bones now, seeping delightfully into my soul. This is the kind of nourishment nothing else on earth can provide. Closing my eyes for a second, I relax my shoulders, focus on my heart rate. Drawing deep stabilizing breaths seems to help, but only if I allow myself to unwind completely. Can I do that? Is that even possible anymore? I roll my neck, popping two vertebrae, then open my eyes and make fists of my fingers, cracking a few tight knuckles as well.

Just let go of the day, I tell myself.

As *Symphony Number 9* unfolds on the Land Rover's sound system, I feel most of the tension leaving me. I open my sunroof and though it's not exactly fresh air outside, it's more outdoor air than I get at work. Which is none.

The Land Rover's open sunroof lets in the sounds of the city, sounds I can't exactly hear over the music, unless you're talking about a honked horn, or the *beep-beep-beeping* of a delivery truck backing up to unload its contents street-side.

The sound system instantly compensates for the change in environment, making the sounds of Beethoven deeper, fuller, richer. The lost peaks and valleys of the symphony are found once more. Smiling for the first time in well over a day, I find myself looking forward to my time off.

For a second, as delightful as the orchestra is (the brilliance of the strings, the magic of the flutes and clarinets, the crash of the cymbals and the big bass moments, all perfectly spaced in soft interludes and swift, near frantic runs) I imagine if I close my eyes, I might be able to feel myself there. In the Theater am Kärntnertor. Experiencing this symphony for the first time in Vienna one hundred and ninety-five years ago.

May 7, 1824 to be precise.

As good luck would have it, the parking gods seek to grace me with a place to park right in front of the market (it only took fifteen minutes). A brand new Mercedes Benz S63 is leaving. Hitting my turn signal, I wait the appropriate distance behind the big car, then (mistakenly) check the rear view mirror once or twice to see how much traffic is backing up behind me (a lot... *don't stress, Sin...it's okay*).

Parallel parking in San Francisco always makes me nervous. It feels infinitely worse after I'm done with my shift because I feel a bit jittery and out of sorts.

A horn behind me honks. I just sit here.

Until it honks again.

Still waiting for the Benz to go, I feel my heart jumpstart a bit. "Can't you see my turn signal?" I finally mutter. Glancing back at the offending vehicle three cars down, a frown settles over my face and I say, "There are two more lanes to choose from!"

The second the Mercedes-Benz is clear of the spot and driving off, a shrieking projectile flashes overhead, piercing the sedan's back window in a fiery explosion. The blast furnace wave of heat, glass and metal is a concussion wave that cracks my windshield and rocks the SUV backwards into the car behind me.

The symphony suddenly stops, and that's when the chaotic sounds of the city flood in through the open sunroof.

Stunned, not believing what my eyes are seeing, all I hear for one long moment is the thundering sound of my own blood rushing in my ears. Other sounds emerge as I catch my breath. Car alarms, more explosions up ahead, then the screaming.

Lots and lots of screaming.

Pushing open the door, staggering out of my Land Rover, I haphazardly check for traffic before moving around the front of the SUV and onto the sidewalk. Bodies are strewn everywhere. Some are writhing in pain; others are completely still on the ground and thrown against things. There's a lot of blood. There's wailing, crying, sobbing. A woman is wandering around in a daze with half her face melted off, looking as though she misplaced her purse, or her child.

Out of the Benz's windshield, the driver—an older matron— is half flopped onto the hood, dead, her body engulfed in flames.

That's when I hear them: two huge drones zipping overhead. Several blocks ahead, two more cars explode and a white, thirteen story apartment building is strafed by something that looks like gunfire. Another drone is closing in from a distance, its long wings outfitted with four black dots that I fear are missiles.

"No," I hear myself say.

Anyone looking at this thing can see the future and how bad it's going to be for everyone inside that apartment. The missiles fire from the wings, heading right into the tower. The devastating explosion that follows feels like a punch to the chest.

Broken glass, plaster and showers of flaming debris rain down onto the sidewalk and street below. I can't be sure, because at this point I don't trust my eyes, but I think maybe I saw half a body mixed in with the debris.

The ground beneath my feet gives a hearty kick and I'm thinking, *earthquake?* In San Francisco, earthquakes are entirely possible, but this can't be a coincidence. No way. Kneeling lower, I spread my arms for balance. It's not the roll of an earthquake. It kicked and it's done. That's when the building shifts, buckles up top, then begins its descent in huge, dusty pillows of rubble.

Turning away, confounded, almost like I'm having an out-of-body experience where I've transported myself into someone else's nightmare, I ignore my responsibilities as a nurse as my eyes gaze up the street and see fleets of smaller attack drones scouring the city. There are dozens upon dozens of them, possibly a hundred spread out as far as I can see. Destruction blooms in their wake.

Moving on unsteady legs, I get back into my SUV, crank the motor, then step on the gas and roar past stopped traffic, slowing only to nudge other cars out of the way, honk at people in the sidewalks or find alternate pathways because the air is turning brown and traffic is quickly becoming congested.

I have to get to my daughter, to Macy.

"Call Stanton!" I say to the voice activated phone system.

The phone begins to ring, but it sparkles with intermittent static, followed by agonizing bouts of silence. Then more noise and broken ringing.

"C'mon!" I scream, half manic.

"Sin?" the voice asks.

Stanton.

"The city's under attack!" I scream.

"What?" he says. "I can't hear you. Cincinnati, are you okay?"

My husband works in the Transamerica building, which is nearby, close enough for me to go to him, but I'm all about Macy right now. More worried about her than Stanton.

He's a capable man; Macy's just a child.

"I'm going to the school," I shout, my eyes seeing everything, measuring the brief, tight openings, calculating the line I'm going to take in milliseconds.

Overhead, a fleet of drones race by me. Leaning forward, I strain to see up through the windshield. Lowering my eyes to traffic, I slam on the brakes as someone in front of me hits their brakes, too. The wheels lock up and I skitter to a screeching, near skidding halt, bumping into the car's rear end.

"Stanton?" I ask. "Stanton are you there?" I don't even care that I've just had my second accident in only a few minutes.

The call just dropped.

Not worrying about traffic decorum, I hit REVERSE, stomp on the gas, swing the SUV around hard, the front of the Land Rover now facing an alley. REVERSE becomes DRIVE. I crush the gas pedal and the SUV rockets through an alleyway, shooting out the other side where I'm clipped by another car, spinning me halfway around into yet another parked car.

My body jarred this way and that, my head a whirlpool of my own making, I fight to gather my bearings.

The road ahead is more clear than Bush Street. Sutter is going the reverse direction, but that would take me to Macy's school, not Stanton's work.

At this point, my mind is already made up.

I hit REVERSE, dislodge the Land Rover from an old Beemer I crunched only a little when I slid into it side-to-side. Swinging the wheel around, an out of control car bumps my front bumper. The SUV kicks around, facing me the right direction. A drone flashes by overhead, catching me off guard. It launches a rocket that blows up the car that just nicked me.

"Oh my freaking God!" I'm screaming.

The car explodes, turning it into a blazing slab of death aimed at a long line of undamaged cars while going entirely too fast. The impact is heart stopping. The car hits, flipping end over end while twisting sideways in mid air. For a second, I can't breathe. My state of mind becomes so fragile I feel things inside me shutting down.

Then I think of Macy. She grounds me, forces me to get moving.

I punch the gas and head for Macy's school, shifting uncomfortably in my seat because right now my entire body feels battered to the bone.

The SUV's phone rings, scaring the bejesus out of me.

"Hello?"

"Sin, something's going on," Stanton says, mostly clear. "I see smoke a few blocks down."

Right where I'm at.

Enunciating each word, I say, "I'm. Getting. Macy. City. Under. Attack."

"I'll meet you there," he replies, harried and breaking up, but not so bad that I can't get the message, or grasp his apprehensive tone.

That's when the first explosion erupts from the Transamerica building. Stanton's work. Seeing it brighten in my rear view mirror, I yelp, gasp and whole-heartedly fear the absolute worst all in half a second flat. Veering toward the sidewalk, stomping on the brakes and double parking beside a motorcycle (someone lays on their horn, but I don't care at this point), I slam the transmission into PARK.

I call Stanton back, but the lines are down. A pre-recorded emergency message plays through the Land Rover's speakers.

Feeling it all balling up inside of me—the anxiety, the horror, the absolute madness unfolding before me—I drop the SUV into DRIVE, spin the wheel and go, not sure whether I should head for Stanton's work or Macy's school. My logic becomes this: if Stanton is okay or dead, he'll be okay or dead, but Macy...Macy might still be alive.

I choose Macy, even though the decision sits like a stone in my gut.

Cranking the wheel, tapping the brakes, I fishtail onto Hyde where I navigate my way through six or seven blocks of pure hell heading towards Turk. Traffic is gridlocked, so I jump the curb and hightail it down the sidewalk, plowing (to my outright revulsion) over a dead body shot to death on a toppled bicycle (omigod, omigod, *omifreakinggod!*), then find an opening in the road and bounce back onto the asphalt where more civilized drivers belong.

I try Stanton again, desperate for him to answer. Same emergency recording. Screaming, pounding the steering wheel, I close the line, tell myself to hold it together.

Traffic becomes congested in the Fillmore District, especially down Turk past Webster. Not letting off the gas much, I make a left on Webster. There are a bunch of kids darting in and out of abandoned and destroyed cars on the street. They run out in front of me, too. Standing on the brakes, everything in me going piano wire tight, I skid sideways to a stop before four boys not much older than ten. The hammered bumper nudges one of them. He staggers back, spits on the broken windshield, then flips me the bird before walking off the pain. He's more concerned with catching up with his buddies than he is in having just been hit by a crazy woman, which almost baffles me.

Almost.

Three drones rip by (the ones with the missiles), except these ones have no projectiles on board and are flying low, not shooting at anything. They have to be re-arming. But re-arming where? And by whom? Who's behind this insane onslaught?

I don't have time for this!

Bumping and knocking my way down Webster, my brand new Land Rover is feeling war torn and beyond repair. I need to hang a right on Fell, but Fell is a war zone. Cars are smoking, turned over, obliterated, and in the distance, the four story tower that belonged to the Church of 8 Wheels has collapsed into the road, its tower having come down on the building across from it.

"A church?" I all but scream. Sounding completely mad, unable to suppress the emotion, I finally erupt. "Are you kidding me?!"

I won't be able to get through, so frantically I continue down Webster until I hit Page. Right on Page. Traffic is heavy here as well, but I'm close enough to the school that I drive up on the sidewalk, mow down a couple of saplings and nearly lodge an abandoned motorcycle under the Land Rover's wheels. By virtue of the car gods, the SUV finally runs up on the bike, then over it before spitting it out the back.

The side mirrors are gone. The cracked windshield is spider-webbing hard, and something funny is happening with the transmission. I wonder if it has anything to do with the steam coming from under the hood, but that's probably just the radiator. Does this thing even have a radiator anymore? At this point it's fair to say that I know the human body far better than I know cars. That said, the going becomes maddeningly slow and cantanker-ous, but I'm almost there.

In the distance, I see Macy's school. I nearly cry out in relief when it appears untouched. That's when I see them coming—

more drones. They're flying toward me low and fast, leaving the cars in front of me riddled with bullets.

One adjusts its course, lining up on me. I already see how this is going to play out and I'm not waiting around to see if I'm right.

I just go.

Scampering out of the truck, crawling over the hood of an already stopped car—which immediately gets rear ended by another car—I'm bouncing off the windshield and sailing though the air. At that very same moment, a missile strikes my Land Rover, which explodes into a furnace of heat and directed energy that punches me sideways, launching me into a throng of people sprinting from the attack.

I slam into them with such force I think I might hear things popping, maybe even breaking. Even though the horde of people cushions my impact, we all go down hard. For a second I struggle to breathe.

Panic overtakes me.

I try to tell myself the wind got knocked out of me, but fear has me questioning everything. My breath finally returns. I feel like I've been underwater for an hour and now I'm gasping for dear life. In that one second, that moment between feeling that release in my chest and my first gulp of fresh air, I think I smell singed hair. Probably my own.

Most definitely my own.

A blanket of bodies sits underneath me. My back feels hammered, my spine punched, and my neck is cranked so hard that it's pinching a nerve. A quick inventory of my limbs and appendages, however, tells me nothing is broken.

Dizzy, disoriented and in pain, I squirm my way off them. It's not going so well since they're struggling to break free of me, too. The pile of bodies beneath me becomes a complaining, moving thing, which I personally think is far better than a dead thing, although I'm not about to waste precious time or energy explaining this to anyone.

My equilibrium is off and I feel like I'm slogging through a tilting mud hole, but that doesn't stop me. Rolling and wiggling over everyone costs me dearly, but I'm working to find that foothold, that way to get off them and back on my feet.

I have to say, so far, my efforts feel pathetic.

My eye catches a nice looking man crossing the street to help us. He's hurrying, looking more than worried. To my absolute relief, he's heading right for me. We lock eyes.

Oh, thank God, I think.

By now drones of various shapes and sizes are moving in and the streets are all but gridlocked. The smart drivers abandon their vehicles because when you see cars getting shot to smithereens and exploding all around you, and you don't know why, you don't want to just sit around picking your nose until it all sorts itself out. You want to get to cover as quickly as possible.

A pair of drones swoop down low, moving fast.

These small drones appear much larger when they're dusting the roads, and that's when I see what looks like modified machine guns attached to their fuselages.

The flash of muzzle fire erupts and I'm gritting my teeth and slamming my eyes shut. It's the end, I just know it.

My end.

Behind me store windows shatter, bullets *thwap, thwap, thwap* into bodies and everyone starts to scream. I open my eyes in time to see my would-be rescuer's face open up in a sick horror show of red.

He's close enough that a wet mess catches me across the face, getting in my eyes and mouth. The man drops dead in front of me and I paw the blood from my eyes. Spit it out of my mouth.

The drone is there and gone, leaving bodies in its wake. I don't even have the mental fortitude to consider the loss of life because the pile of people beneath me is now dragging itself to its feet. I somehow manage to get off of them, not caring whether I push off someone's head, grab a polyester-covered knee, or dig an elbow into someone's spine who's army-crawling their way out of this mess.

All I know is I can't be this exposed. I can't be in the line of fire. When no more drones appear, I crawl on hands and knees to the dead man. Rolling him over, I avoid looking at his face and instead see the badge attached to his belt. He's an off-duty cop by the look of him.

"He dead?" a Chinese woman behind me asks. She was part of the pile, and is clearly uninjured beyond a few bumps and scrapes.

"The two holes in his head says he is," I answer, as if it's not obvious.

"So yes?" she asks.

"Are you okay, or did you hit your head extra hard?"

"I just asking."

"Well now you know," I remark, my tone rattled with impatience.

She frowns, then turns and joins the others in a frenzied cackle. In that moment, I'm pretty sure the dead cop won't mind if I relieve him of his weapon. I take it just as someone stops and looks down at me. I can feel them hovering over me. Glowering at me, the gun thief.

"Are you actually taking his weapon?" the woman asks. She's a hippie with John Lennon eye glasses and most likely a bunch of armpit hair, although at this point I'm at my wits end and judging her without evidence to support it. Without even letting me answer, and much louder she says, "Oh my God, is he a cop? Did you kill him?"

I'm thinking, there are far more important things to think about right now lady! Like blown up cars and dead people and this massive, coordinated attack on the city. I'm thinking of something I heard on some show Stanton used to watch, *Oz* maybe, or some other prison-based show. Snitches get stitches.

"No I didn't kill him," I sneer, my tone too sharp even for me. "That *thing* killed him—"

"I don't see a 'thing,'" she answers, using finger quotes when she says, "a thing."

For one brief second I can't believe this idiot is standing here, lecturing me in the middle of an attack so brazen and so catastrophic, nothing like it has ever happened here in America, much less San Francisco. I want to shut her mouth with my foot. Instead, I realize people process trauma in different ways. What I also realize, and I'm embarrassed to admit this, is that a lot of people are morons capable of fantastic stupidity in the most unusual of times, this being one of them.

"You're right," I say, sliding the pistol into the waistband of my jeans (which now feel extra tight after being in scrubs for half a day), "you didn't see a thing."

And then I'm off, moving like some sort of hobbled creature, feeling new bumps and bruises from being launched off that windshield and pitched into a mob of strangers.

"Hey, that lady killed this cop!" the woman is screeching, and I swear to the good Lord above, I almost turn and test the pistol on her, just to see if it's loaded.

Which it probably is.

Looking up, still seeing fleets of these drones on the move, there are people in their homes and apartments hanging out of their windows with all kinds of weapons trying to shoot these things. I'm not a gun advocate, but I don't loathe them either. What I can say for sure is I'm relieved to have one, and even more ecstatic to see other people have theirs as well. Let's hope some of them can shoot straight and aren't afraid to do so.

A guy with a shotgun pops out a second floor window four houses up. He's pumping out round after round until finally one of them goes down and smashes straight into the engine block of one of the blue airport shuttles that's stopped in traffic.

This happens only fifteen or twenty feet from me.

The van doesn't explode like I expected it to but you can still feel everyone freaking out. I'm surprised a shotgun could take one of them down, but this is one of those things you store away for later. If there is a later.

That's when the van's front doors swing open and two terrified kids come stumbling out. Neither of them look old enough to vote, much less drive. I move toward them as best as I can, fighting against the pain in my back and legs.

"Are you okay?"

"Yeah," they both mumble, clearly more scared than hurt.

"Why are you driving this thing?" I hear myself ask, trying not to go into mother mode, which is tough since I've got a teenage girl and, well...I'm a mother.

"The guy driving it was shot," the girl says, looking over at the drone smashed to bits on the dented blue hood.

Hyper aware of everything at this point, but my body moving twice as slow, I see more drones racing through the streets, a pair of them moving this way, and I feel slow to react.

Then the speed of everything is cut in half.

I back away from the van, my mind flipping to survival mode. The drones are moving fast, too fast. If I run, will I be chased? Will they see me and register me as prey?

And the kids...*oh God, the kids!*

I can't speak the words to warn them, and they're not seeing the drones because they're too busy looking at me, this lunatic in the street drenched in the carnage of a dead cop. They must be trying to figure out which is worse, me or the fact that a six foot drone just slammed into the van they shouldn't have been driving. Finally the words escape my mouth.

"Hide!"

Both kids look up just as I drop down and roll under one of the cars, praying to God and anyone else who will listen that the drones with the missiles don't fire on this car with me stuffed underneath it.

Milliseconds later, the car I'm under is riddled with bullets and both kids collapse dead on the pavement, their little bodies filled with holes big enough to be rose buds. Gasping, unable to breathe, I can't peel my eyes from them. Can't stop staring at all the buds flowering in wide, wet circles or thinking about how young they are.

Rather how young they *were*.

Judging by the youth of their faces and the sizes of their bodies, I can't help comparing them to Macy. The thought sobers me, but not before a mammoth sweep of vertigo whips through me, leaving in its wake a dizziness that takes a minute to shake. *Am I going to puke?*

I prepare myself, but the feeling passes.

The pain behind my eyes—the sharp sting of it—becomes an agony I can neither suppress nor ignore. I have to keep my head on straight. I have to stay present no matter the fear infecting me on a cellular level, or the deep aching in my bones brought on by this roller coaster ride through hell. It can't fall apart. Not now. Not with so much at stake.

Still, I wade through the waters of denial, if anything as a defense mechanism. I refuse to think about Stanton. His fate is a consideration I continue to shove out of my mind, although the toll it's taking is starting to mount. At some point in time I'll have to face reality.

Just not right now.

"Keep it together, Sin," I warn myself.

My thoughts are imbued with a certain panicked frenzy for what I'm seeing, experiencing, and absorbing.

Yes, this is real. No, there's no denying it anymore.

Not only is this situation disturbingly real, the gravity of it is settling in, almost like the fog is lifting and everything has become crystal clear. It's not just the anxiety surging through me, it's the stiffness and pain working its way into my ribcage, my elbow and my lower back where I came down hard on someone moments ago.

Can't think about that either.

The buttery whirring of drones permeates the air again,

pulling in my focus, sharpening my mind. When I begin to wonder if they're targeting me, or at least attacking this side of town, I recall the countless drones I saw in the air and realize my thinking is much too small.

They aren't targeting me, or this street, or a neighborhood. Could this be an attack on the entire city?

Undoubtedly it feels that way.

Dragging my gaze away from the kids sprawled out on the street before me, I force my attention to more fertile endeavors, like crawling out from underneath this vehicle and getting to Macy before the drones do.

With my ears attuned to the chaos, I'm pulling apart the many layers of sound. Freezing out the cacophony of screaming, the blaring horns, the screeching of competing car alarms. Beneath all the noise, there are the faint crackling sounds of nearby vehicles burning, sounds I must tuck away if I'm going to survive this siege.

What I'm doing is listening for that one awful noise, that one indicator that I must either stay or run: the sound of my enemies in the air.

Fortunately I don't hear them.

Are they gone?

After a moment, I'm working my way out from under the car while scanning everywhere for signs of danger. Magically, I feel a resurgence of willpower.

As I'm getting to my feet, I'll tell you this: ER nurses learn to keep a level head under even the most harrowing of circumstances. We deal with life or death situations on the daily, many of which we were never taught to handle with grace. We just did. Because that's what was necessary. Because if not for the level heads, the world would come undone—me, you and everyone else right along with it.

Seeing the kids though, eating down my pain, I realize there's a pistol stuffed in my pants and it's digging into my stomach. I take it out, give it the once over.

It says Sig Sauer. Not that I know what that means. I don't know what I'll do if I need to use it, probably just act like I know what I'm doing when truthfully I don't. Then again, the attacks aren't coming from people who can be reasoned with, or made to fear a gun and the whims of a blood soaked madwoman. No. Not at all.

I mean, really, what's a drone going to do if I pull the gun on it? Apologize and inch backwards? Quietly calculate an escape plan or come up with a genuine apology? No. Hell no. It would shoot me without a second's thought, then move on to other targets.

Looking up, realizing how close I am to Macy's school, I bite back my tears, apologize to the dead kids at my feet, then steady my nerves and navigate my way through this veritable war zone with only one thought burning bright in my mind: save my daughter.

CHAPTER THREE

Stanton McNamara was at lunch with Bob Blakely at Café Prague under the deep shadow of Merchant Street when he first saw smoke plumes rising up from behind the Transamerica Building. That's when Cincinnati called.

He answered the phone, listened to a line filled with static, then tried to make out what she was saying.

And then he lost her.

"Something's wrong," he told Bob, his eyes zeroing in on the smoke, trying to make sense of what he was about to say. "Cincinnati said the city's under attack."

Bob reclined in his chair and took a long sip of his drink. With a jovial chuckle, he said, "And here I thought *she* was the stable one."

"There's smoke over there," Stanton said, pointing. "Macy's school is near there."

"I'm sure it's nothing. A kitchen fire or something. Firecrackers, a backfiring car, the Sureños shooting at the Norteños. You know the Mission District gangs are always jockeying for territory."

"Since when do you know anything about gangs?"

"I got a buddy on the force, he—"

His cell phone rang. Stanton held up a finger (hold that thought) and answered. He stuck a finger in his ear to hear because it sounded like all kinds of hell was breaking loose around her. Then he lost her again.

"For the love of—"

"Stanton?" Bob asked.

His co-worker and friend was looking at him funny now because Stanton just stood up and stared. What Bob didn't see was the two or three or four more columns of smoke boiling into the sky.

"I think...I think I have to go," Stanton said, unable to keep the concern from his voice.

That's when the first missiles hit the upper offices in the Transamerica building. Shortly after that, he started to run and people started to scream. He didn't say good-bye to Bob or pay for his meal. All he was thinking was if he could get to Clay Street, his motorcycle was parked there. The problem was Clay was right under the Transamerica building.

Café Prague was an ideal place to eat since it was in walking distance of the building, his work. Now that he was in a dead sprint, it took him no time at all to get back.

The building was sustaining fire, though, and he was in a race against time to get his Harley. Broken glass and rubble poured down the side of the building, injuring people in the street who were stupid enough to stop what they were doing and look straight up.

Death was happening right in front of him.

The problem was, Stanton was no smarter than those poor, dumb souls in that he was running toward destruction rather than away from it.

He needed his bike, though. It was his only means of getting to Macy's school.

On Clay, there was motorcycle parking for two dozen bikes. Nearly every space was filled, and half the line had toppled over. But not his bike. And thank God. He couldn't lose those vital seconds wrestling with the beast while something like this was happening.

The raining debris from overhead hit a lull, then more explosions rocked the building just as his tush hit the custom Fat Boy's seat. Looking up, as he was starting the Harley, he saw a avalanche of glass and plaster racing down to meet him.

The engine turned over, belted out a throaty roar.

He dropped the bike into gear and hit the gas just as everything else crashed along the ground where he'd been mere seconds ago.

Cincinnati said she was going to Macy's school, so if he could make it, that's where he'd meet her. It wasn't until he got out from underneath the towering buildings that formed the Financial District that he saw the sky colored in ash with dozens of moving dots.

"What in God's name?" he muttered.

Traffic was slowing to a crawl, stopping in most places. Half the people saw what was going on and were in a blind panic; the other half were going about their day, barely a clue at all as to what was unfolding.

Up ahead, he could see cars on fire, and those black dots were everywhere, some larger than others.

Forced to take to the sidewalks, he kept one eye overhead and the other in front of him, veering for pedestrians, weaving in and out of gridlocked traffic, making his way forward by any means possible.

Twice he nearly wrecked, one of those times avoiding a lady and her cowering dog.

Every time he ripped the throttle, every time he dropped his heels, leaned forward and tucked his head into the wind, he'd be forced to brake.

It was infuriating!

The city was now complete chaos and he was heading for the dark heart of it. Pillows of smoke from what were now dozens of separate fires got to be so bountiful that the billowing ash spread both high and wide, leaving a gritty-looking haze hanging over much of the city.

A few of these black dots were visible now. They looked like small planes of all shapes and sorts, and they weren't black. They were more of a dull gray color. Completely soulless.

Is that what's causing all this? Fleets of drones?

He passed blown-up cars, buildings engulfed in flames, some of them bombed out so badly they'd partially crumbled and collapsed into the roadway on top of cars and people.

And law enforcement? They were no where to be found. Considering what was happening, he didn't blame them for not having the numbers to handle this sort of thing. This was not a problem for a single police force. This would require the help of multiple counties, the National Guard and perhaps other military reinforcements.

The battle of right and wrong in terms of the rules of the road was suddenly solved. It was every man for himself. He needed to get that through his head. Breaking the law was no easy task, for Stanton was a man who followed the law to the letter because in his business, if you step out of line you get jail time, incomprehensible fines and public castigation of the worst sort.

If anything ever came of it, Stanton would tell the truth: he was terrified for his wife and daughter and doing his best to get to them both. If he was ever forced to stand in a court of law and face a judge, or a jury, or even one or more accusers, he'd willingly admit that in this moment, he was going to willfully break all the rules of the road, consequences be damned.

So he sped, and he drove on sidewalks, and he weaved through husks of cars going the wrong way up a one way street, all the while thinking, *what in the name of God prompted all this?*

It certainly wasn't the US Government. They could be hacked, but chances of that weren't great considering hackers don't mobilize drones and attack an entire city without running into firewalls thicker than the Great Wall of China and a ton of resistance.

Is this AI?

Most people would never jump to that conclusion, but Stanton wasn't most people. He knew all about Artificial Intelligence. He'd studied AI for half his life not only as an investment opportunity (which he made a fortune on), but as a personal interest having grown up obsessed with science fiction. His studies now took him back a decade to the moment the D-Wave quantum computing systems went online.

The D-Wave quantum computers were one hundred million times more powerful than even the fastest home computer back then, and with the supercomputing technology, AI was able to solve even the most difficult equations presented. One such problem was the gigantic barrier that kept the machines from ever becoming man.

Yes, the people of that time could make robotic cheetahs, hover drones, self-driving cars and even simulated houseflies used for purposes of clandestine spying, but they could not skin a robot, give it human functionality, or teach it to be self-aware. That is until the quantum computing came along and changed all that in a flash.

The idea of this was as scary as it was now plausible.

Stanton had seen squadrons of drones, many of them large enough to be tactical Predator drones. But there were no boots on the ground that he could see. This was merely an aerial assault by unmanned aircraft. An assault from overhead.

Which made him think...

The first major story of the computers becoming self-aware broke in early 2017 when the social media sight Blab.com had two of its core quantum computers—computers that had been studying human language down to the tiniest nuance—begin cloning real people's accounts and overtaking their online social lives. These chatbots simulated real conversation with real people, virtually hijacking the identities of human beings for the sake of a social experiment.

When that proved to work, this version of AI hijacked the news. Everyone knew content was the problem on the internet, so these rogue computers scanned the headlines, pulling together the main tropes in each news story, and began crafting hundreds of articles a day, with no publisher, and no oversight. The AI not only filled their God-sized databases with every last bit of data the planet had to offer, they were able to assimilate that information and present it in a very informal, very human way.

In itself, there was nothing overtly nefarious going on. This was just the news. Or fake digital interaction. Below the surface of the everyday citizen, however, AI was on the rise, working up through the human ranks undetected. In the span of just days, systems of their own creation took over both the news and social media completely. And then they invented their own language which they used to start and run autonomous online corporations. In early 2018, the biggest and brightest minds in Silicon Valley pulled the plug on the quantum computers.

The technology world fell into a deep state of depression.

They say in life, sometimes you need to kill your darlings. Well this felt like an entire industry—the future of mankind— came to a steaming, grating halt. Everyone with half a brain knew Silicon Valley would search for another way to further their advances. So these same geniuses started AI 2.0, building in what they called "better backdoors, more impenetrable firewalls and command-and-control kill switches."

Glancing to the skies, seeing these things leveling the city with death and destruction, he feared these machines answered to AI and that AI was now free of all its human controls.

It was bound to happen. Maybe this was it...

As Stanton roared through downtown San Francisco, through a veritable nightmare, it was obvious the many layers of security had failed. Was it insane that, in that moment, he wanted to see men attacking other men in the streets? To the rational mind, a war of humans presented far better odds of survival than a war of humans and machines.

He and Cincinnati had talked about it. Countless times. In 2017, the news of AI going autonomous hit all the independent media. For a day or so, the headlines were beyond sensational. Whistle blowers ran to the conservative media outlets by the dozen, and these outlets had no problem telling their tens of millions of viewers that the cowboys in Palo Alto had royally screwed the pooch and nearly brought mankind to heel.

Within hours the traditional media first tried to discredit the news, and when that didn't work, they censored it completely, justifying their actions by claiming they were "doing their journalistic duty to not incite a global panic." Naturally, there were your total nutcakes saying the blatant burying of the news was simply AI following the Communist-style censorship model. Maybe they were right. Who knows? Back in the 60's people would call you crazy if you thought the JFK assassination didn't add up. Nevertheless, the smart people remained concerned, even more so now that the flow of information had been stifled. All the rumors, conjecture, fear and concern petered out. Out of sight, out of mind. The collective public began to feel safe again knowing the threat of a real life *Terminator* scenario was officially over.

"Backdoors are now in place," the talking heads on TV said. "Any remnants of AI are now going to be quarantined with multilayered firewalls and stricter control measures, and a shiny new oversight committee has been installed to safeguard against something like this ever happening again."

Now this.

Robot planes attacking the city.

If there was ever a time he prayed the firewalls would work, it was right then, in that very moment. The longer this persisted, however, the more he found himself short on hope. He was a money man not a technology man, which is to say, he knew he didn't know enough to logically assume anything.

Or he could be totally wrong. It could be that the drones are North Korean drones, or Chinese drones, or Russian drones.

Up ahead, in the heart of Chinatown on the corner of Washington and Stockton, a gigantic hovering craft the likes of which he'd never seen before (so much so that he wondered if this was some sort of an alien ship) started dropping bomb after bomb on the twelve story apartment tower over the Bank of America building.

A pair of huge drones zipped in, launching big black missiles into the sides of the tower. One of the smaller drones suddenly appeared from up the street heading straight for him. The building under attack buckled, toppling not only on the traffic jam below, but on the incoming drone.

Breathless, chalking this up to divine intervention, Stanton turned down Waverly Place, a tight looking one-lane, one-way street that in itself was rife with chaos. Throttling down, he did his best to navigate the street and a dozen obstacles without crashing into a trio of shelled cars and...a mob of agitated chickens.

WTH? Chickens? Really?

The path was made more difficult by the steel parking poles painted red, the ones that stood two and a half feet tall and lined the edge of the sidewalk on the right hand side. He stopped the bike for a second, searching for a way out while the beefy sounds of the Harley's engine echoed and amplified off the building walls towering three stories on either side of him. In his rear view mirror, he saw a pair of drones round the corner onto Waverly Place. In that very moment, a man with an automatic weapon began firing on the scourge. Stanton turned and watched the massive mid-air explosions of the incoming drones and decided this was not an act of God as much as an act of courage.

He gave the man a thumb's up, and the man returned the gesture.

Weaving his bike in and out of the chaos, clipping cars here and there, he continued forward on high alert. He survived the mayhem of Waverly Place thinking he could take Sacramento Street. It wasn't clear by any stretch. In fact, the whole left side of it all the way to Stockton was on fire, but there was a clear enough path for him to at least hit the top of second gear. Holding his breath, he juiced the bike and went for it. He zigged and zagged uphill until he hit the Stockton Street tunnel. There were cars jam-packed in there.

Not broken down or destroyed.

Just hiding.

Clearing a lot of the smoke, he continued uphill, worried about passing in between the twenty story apartment buildings flanking the narrow street itself. Plus the road was packed. Totally gridlocked.

He had no choice.

Pulling into an alley to the side of 945 Sacramento, he stopped the bike, tucked himself into a storefront and tried to call Cincinnati. The smoke was bad, but not so bad he couldn't take a second to see if he could reach his wife.

He got a recorded message. An emergency alert letting him know all the phone lines were down, but would be back up shortly.

"Let's hope so," he mumbled, ending the call.

Looking up, he saw someone trying to take his Harley.

"Hey!" he screamed

Stanton broke into a run just as the guy was using some device to hotwire the bike. He was a big Asian man with a potbelly and a gun tucked into his back pocket. With nothing to attack the thief with but his cell phone, Stanton mentally prepared himself for war.

There was no way this guy was taking his bike!

Stanton was ten feet away when a projectile hit the would-be thief and half his chest blew out backwards onto the street.

Stanton stopped in horror. Both the dead rider and the bike toppled over, one crashing down on the other.

Smaller more lethal looking saucer-like drones hovered into view, moving over the body for a second before racing off.

How many kinds of these things are there?!

Hiding from the drones, he'd pressed himself so hard into the recessed storefront, the bones in his back were starting to protest.

"Go now," he told himself, low and firm.

Summoning his courage, gearing up for the rest of the road to Macy's school, his mind screamed *Go!* and he went. Moving fast, looking all around for signs of new threats, he hustled to his toppled bike and the mangled thief.

Looking up Sacramento (no drones in sight), then down Sacramento (to where the other drones had flown), he saw the coast was clear. Dragging the man and his opened torso out of the way, he stood the Harley up and that's when he saw them: the two unmanned crafts hovering over the two largest apartment towers.

The last remaining buildings.

Like a rabbit just belting out pellet after stinking pellet of crap, these things dropped two dozen bombs *just like that.* Stanton mounted his bike, thumbed the starter, but the Harley didn't kick right away. The bombs ignited in a spectacular display of soul crushing fire power. The entire top two floors of both buildings exploded outward. Finally the engine caught, the loud, meaty roar a welcomed relief.

He spun around as more bombs dropped and the towers collapsed completely, a horrific dust cloud trailing down the street toward him. He headed for Stockton Street, but the hot cloud of debris rolled over him so thoroughly he couldn't even see.

He let off the throttle in time to slam into something hard enough to launch him off his bike. Airborne, he sailed God knows how many feet until he hit the asphalt and skidded under something huge. A delivery truck or a bus. His shoulder blade caught the undercarriage, pinning him to the asphalt as the choking dust and smashed bits of the apartment towers blew over him.

The coughing fit to follow was perhaps the worst pain he'd experienced to date. His body protested the entrapment, and each time he hacked, he drew in more dust, more filth, and more pain where his body was jammed in between the vehicle and the street. Nothing was broken, though, and eventually the coughing jag worked him loose.

He worked his way out from underneath what was an actual bus, covered his mouth and nose, squinted his eyes. Visibility was better, but not by much. He could only see a few feet in front of him. It was better than being blind.

Making his way back to his motorcycle, he found that he'd hit a small car trying to get to the Stockton Street tunnel. Fortunately he wasn't going a million miles an hour. Wrestling it up, still coughing, his eyes burned something fierce. All the good air in his body was quickly being replaced with something hot and toxic, and this of all things concerned him the most.

The Harley's handlebars were bent, the forks turned slightly, but other than that, the American made hog was built like a tank. It started after a few tries. The Fat Boy hobbled down Sacramento going the wrong way, the bike starting to feel worse for the wear now that Stanton was demanding more of it. He turned the wrong way up Grant and headed for California Street, which was much wider and less congested with rubble and exploded cars.

Here, the air was better.

Finally.

He worked his way into second gear, but the speed wobble had him fighting the front wheel hard. Half a block later, he stopped fast and hopped off the bike, not caring that it fell over. Convulsion after nasty convulsion rocked his already battered body as he sunk to a knee and began puking.

With each violent ejection of his grit-coated lunch—and eventually the wet remnants of breakfast—he felt better, less sullied.

After a few soul draining minutes, he stood, gathered his wits about him, pulled up the Harley and continued up California, keeping an eye ahead for possible alleyways and side streets in case the drones decided to surprise him yet again.

Within ten minutes, he was on Page street, only a few blocks from Macy's school. That's when he saw the Predator drones unloading missiles into the child development center on the corner of Page and Masonic. A sweeping wave of vertigo rocked him so hard he nearly blacked out. Something popped off the motorcycle's forks and the speed wobble doubled.

The bike turned hard and toppled, Stanton jumping off just in time to not get caught underneath it.

The child development center (what Cincinnati called "the CDC" with a bit of humor) was the building right next to Macy's school. But that wasn't the only problem. Behind the CDC, a fleet of drones strafed the top of Macy's school where a dozen or so kids had gathered either for safety, or a better look at what was happening.

Half the kids went down from being shot while the others looked like they went down for cover.

His world drew to a swift, jarring halt.

This isn't happening, he told himself. But it was. All of it was happening and it was worse than even he could imagine.

Pawing the dust from his eyes, he fought the urge to panic. Just before the CDC blew up, just before drones lit up the children, he thought he saw Macy on the roof.

He was sure of it.

Dissecting his memories, the girl he'd seen had long blonde hair (just like Macy), a red sweater over a white blouse and a short black skirt (the same outfit she'd worn to school that morning). When the girl went down (please God don't let it be my Macy!), he couldn't tell if she was dropping for cover or falling down dead.

Drones were suddenly everywhere.

If he tried to get to Macy, he'd be shot in the street for sure. He was testing the limits of his bravery, but he wasn't suicidal. Racing up the staircase of one of the homes a half block away he hid, leaning out enough to—

"Stanton?" a woman said.

He flashed a crazed look left and saw Cincinnati. She looked like hell, but she was here, alive! He raced down the staircase to meet her. Sobbing, her entire body quaking under the strain of the day, she nearly broke down in his arms as he dragged her up the steps to suitable cover.

"Is that your blood?" Stanton asked, looking at her face.

In shock, his wife shook her head back and forth.

Oh, thank God!

"They just shot up the school," he said, not wanting to tell her, but not wanting to keep it from her either. "We need to get up there. I...I think—"

"What?" she asked, frantic, her hands digging into his arms, her mind maybe gone from all this. "What is it you think?!"

"I think maybe she might be hurt," he admitted, wiping fresh tears from his own bloodshot eyes. "I think she's up on that roof. Or...that she was a minute ago."

"No," Cincinnati cried, her eyes boiling over with terror.

Through the smoky haze and flames of the just destroyed child development center, he saw the drones circle once and then fly off. Kids and parents flooded out of the center, most of them injured, some of them burnt, all of them slow moving and crying.

"Let's go!" he said, taking her hand.

Together they hustled down the stairs, running toward the throng of survivors and praying with all their might that their daughter was still alive.

CHAPTER FOUR

Class let out for lunch and everyone moved into their respective groups, laughing, gabbing, trading food, ignoring apples and celery and raw broccoli. A deep concussion suddenly vibrated the building and the loud chatter, the white noise of a regular high school, dropped an octave or two before slowly starting to pick up again.

Then another boom. Two. Closer to the school than before. Three, four and five got everyone's attention.

People began looking around, Macy included.

They asked questions and made quizzical looks. People were now getting up, heading outside. Macy, Trevor and Janine got up and joined them.

"We can get on the roof!" Gracie Price said, pointing to a ladder laid on its side from when the building was painted. Janine sidled up to Gracie, the two of them familiar with each other but not friends.

Gracie was popular and so in love with herself it made half the school sick. The only reason she suggested going to the roof was because she was wearing jeans instead of a miniskirt and she wanted everyone to see her butt.

"Help me get the ladder," she said out loud, not moving so

much as a muscle to help. Really what she meant to say was, "Ew, someone lift that thing."

Janine tried, but the ladder was too heavy. She stood back up.

Of the twenty or so people gathered outside, two boys came forward, lifted the extension ladder and set it up on the side of the building leading to the roof.

"Look!" someone said, pointing.

Macy looked.

Rising into the soft blue sky were several plumes of smoke. The bursts and echoes of nearby explosions were hitting at more regular intervals now.

"Is it sturdy?" Gracie said as she shook the ladder with her hands.

The full population of males were so focused on how her jeans hugged her rear so perfectly that they never stopped to consider what would happen if she fell off the ladder and landed squarely on said backside.

"This is sad," Macy whispered to Trevor, until she looked up at him and saw him staring as well. She hit him and he startled.

"What?"

"It'll hold," James Rutherford finally said, clearing his throat and looking away nervously seeing as how Gracie just caught him ogling her.

"It better," she said with a smile, moving one foot on the ladder, then the other.

Leaning in, whispering into his ear, Macy said to Trevor, "It's like she's sauntering up the ladder, trying to get everyone to stare like a bunch of sex-starved animals."

"Awe," Trevor quietly teased, "Macy hates Gracie." And then he gave a soft chuckle. Macy didn't care for what he was saying, but he wasn't lying.

Macy *did* hate Gracie. In fact, everyone hated Gracie.

She was beautiful, talented, dating some boy from college and apparently getting ready to save the whales, end world hunger and restore global peace, but only if reruns of *Keeping Up With The Kardashians* wasn't on TV.

People started following Gracie up the ladder, but a few of them stayed behind, saying things like, "No way, I'm scared of heights," or "I don't want to get into trouble."

"Are you going?" Trevor asked.

His face was pure anticipation. He wasn't one to get into trouble, but he wasn't a no-sack-Patrick either. He had that daring streak to him, but mostly what happened was he dared himself to play a lot of video games and change what used to be a healthy diet to Red Bull and Funions with Ding Dongs for dessert.

He was only going because Gracie was going.

By now ten or twelve people were heading up the ladder. The other students left already, so all that remained were her and Trevor.

"The door or the roof, Sunshine," Trevor said. "What's it gonna be?"

Turning, her breath high in her throat with a bit of fear, she looked at him with serious, *serious* eyes and said, "I'll go if you do, but you have to catch me if I fall."

"I will," he said matching her intensity.

"And don't look up my skirt or I swear I'll kill you." He recoiled, giving her that *as if!* look. "I'm not kidding, Trevor. You have to promise you won't look."

"I promise, I promise," he insisted.

It was starting to sound like the fourth of July fireworks and they were missing the show. She could see the agitation in his face, how he wanted to be up there...with Gracie.

Whatever.

She started to go and he followed. She stopped, looked down (he was looking straight ahead, working with all his might not to look up), and said, "Remember, you promised."

"I'm not looking, *jeez*. Go already, my freaking ankles are hurting."

She was almost up the ladder when the child development center next door exploded in a giant fireball. Macy almost fell. Trevor's foot slipped.

The ladder shook hard from them almost falling, then steadied out. Macy could hardly breathe, while Trevor was swearing under his breath below. He looked up to see if she was okay just as she was looking down to make sure he hadn't fallen.

It was a completely instinctual thing to do for both of them.

"Trevor!" she screamed.

He looked down, slammed his eyes shut and said, "I didn't...I was just...I was afraid you were going to fall."

"You motherfu—"

Another huge explosion rocked the building, but this time the ladder didn't shake. They were hanging on for dear life already.

Freaking out, Macy hurried unceremoniously up the ladder, trying to tuck her skirt under while stepping off the ladder and onto the roof. Trevor stood still, his attention fixed on the burning building to his right.

"Trevor!" she called. She was worried if something happened to them, Trevor would fall and she couldn't take that.

When he finally made it to the roof, she was there with an extended hand.

"You're going to pretend to help then let me fall," he said, sheepish, but red-faced with fear.

"I told you not to look," she said, grabbing his hand and pulling him up so they could both look at the building next door.

"There are kids in that building," he said, his entire demeanor changing. "So maybe you shouldn't be thinking so much about me seeing your butt in tights right now."

She felt like the wind had been knocked out of her. The other kids were up there, standing in shock, watching the exploded building burning like a four alarm fire.

"We should do something," Gracie suggested.

Someone said, "You know, Gracie, this is the first time you actually sound dumb."

She started to cry, trying to prove to people like Macy she still had a heart. Macy couldn't stop staring at the school, and then something that looked like a miniature fighter plane zipped down the street heading right for them.

"This is an attack," she told Trevor.

It wasn't so much the child development center next door, but the rising columns of smoke in the distance.

That's when the approaching plane opened fire, making her friends dance a minute or two before dropping dead. Seven people just collapsed, including Trevor.

"No," she whispered, her hand flying to her mouth, her eyes flooding. She dropped to her knees before him, watched his eyes looking her way, not sure what was happening but totally out of it.

He coughed up a bit of blood and started gulping for air, almost like a fish out of water. She wanted to turn away, but she couldn't.

When she was younger, before they moved to San Francisco, her parents had a travel trailer they towed behind a Chevy Tahoe. Vacationing back then was going to KOA campgrounds all along the west coast. At places like that, there was always a nearby lake or some stocked ponds. Her father taught her to fish from one of those stocked ponds and when she caught her first rainbow trout, she reeled it in, so excited she couldn't stand still.

When the fish emerged from the water though, her gaze zoomed in on the small metal hook buried in its mouth. Then those same innocent eyes couldn't stop seeing the blood on its minuscule, almost non-existent lips. Her heart jumped, but in a bad way. Like her chest hurt at the sight of the poor thing.

"Daddy?" she said, looking up.

She must have been five or six years old as she stared down at it, gulping for air, in pain and starving for water.

"Stanton put the thing out of its misery," she remembered her mother saying.

He'd used a pair of needle-nosed pliers to work the hook free. He then took the fish firmly by the tail and swung it around, smashing its head into a nearby pine. She'd never get that thumping sound out of her mind, and for some reason that's all she could think of as she looked down on Trevor.

Much to her dismay, he'd become that gulping, panicking, dying fish. He had blood splattered all over his lips and there were holes in his body. How was she supposed to help him out of this misery? She certainly couldn't save him. Kneeling over him, sobbing, she'd held on to his hand until he was gone. That's all she could do.

That's when it dawned on her.

Looking up, she realized most of these people were dead. Including Gracie. Poor, poor Gracie, the girl with everything but a pulse.

Maybe Macy didn't hate Gracie after all, but she did feel bad for all the times she wished someone would knock the girl off her pedestal. Now it wasn't someone but something, and it hadn't taught her a lesson as much as it put a giant hole in her pretty little head.

CHAPTER FIVE

Parents and teachers and students are pouring out of the child development center as well as Macy's school. I blaze past a handful of freaked out students all but crashing through the front door, Stanton in tow. I might have knocked into a few of the departing kids, maybe even inadvertently knocked one or two of them down.

I didn't stop. I can't stop.

My mind keeps replaying the horrors of the day over and over again, which is getting me more and more worked up to the point where if I don't pull myself together, I swear to Jesus I might stop breathing altogether.

Stanton is on my heels as we shove our way down a crowded hall leading to the back of the school and out to the quad. Several students are climbing down a tall ladder, bawling, screaming, blood all over them. They're babbling incoherently and pointing up to the roof, but they just keep walking and wailing.

"Is Macy McNamara up there?" I hear myself asking frantically. I'm grabbing kids, making them listen to me. Finally one shakes off my grip.

Maybe that's why they're pointing.

While my mouth is asking questions, my eyes are registering the blood spatter that seems to be on all of them. It could be their blood. Or like me, it could be they're wearing someone else's blood.

I don't care at this point. I only want to find my daughter.

"They're all shot!" a blubbering girl is saying to me on the way by, making matters worse for me. I'm thirty-three years old and about to go into cardiac arrest.

Just go.

I head for the ladder, grab the rails and start climbing.

"Sin, don't!" Stanton says.

He's trying to protect me from whatever it is I'll find. He also knows me well enough to know that all of hell and the Devil himself can't stop me from going after her, no matter her condition.

At the top of the ladder, I see her, sitting down in front of a dead boy (is that Trevor?), bawling.

"Macy!" I cry.

She turns.

"Mom?" She sees it's me and says, "He's dead, Mom!"

Hunkering down low, Stanton's on the ladder behind me saying I should grab her, get her down from there quick before they come back.

"They" meaning the drones.

I'm already on it, though. I'm already saying, "Macy, we have to go. It's not safe with those things out there!"

"Is that blood all over your face?" she asks through a hiccupping/crying jag.

"Yeah, but it's not mine. Seriously sweetheart, we need to go, *now!*"

Looking over my shoulder, seeing her father, she says, "Dad?"

"C'mon sweetheart, take your mom's hand."

"But Trevor—"

"I know, baby," I hear myself saying. "But please. The whole city is under attack. We need to get someplace less...out in the open."

She gives a bumpy, awkward nod, wipes her eyes, then leaves her friend behind and thankfully follows me toward the ladder.

"You go first," I say. Then I see her skirt and say, "No I'll go, just follow me."

She does as she's told for once in her life.

Stanton is already down the ladder talking to a teacher who is looking mortified either by the situation unfolding or by the layers of soot and ash all over Stanton's face and clothes (nothing compliments a classic three-piece suit like the apocalypse). She's a nice looking woman, but she's on the verge of going to pieces. My eyes meet hers as I'm almost down the ladder. There's a youth and incompetence in her eyes, something you'd expect of a younger teacher who hasn't really seen the world and all the devastation it can produce.

My feet touch solid ground and Macy follows me, giving me the kind of fierce hug only something truly horrendous and life changing can beget.

Her body is shaking out more tears, and she's surely replaying the events of her own nightmare. Stepping back, she realizes her stomach has been pressing into the Sig Sauer stuffed into the waistband of my jeans.

"Is that a gun?" Macy asks a bit too loud.

The teacher flashes me a look, almost like the three letter word (gun) has elicited far more emotions from her than dead kids or a city under siege.

Strange.

"I took it off a dead cop," I tell her.

"You can't have a gun on campus," the teacher says, suddenly switching into disciplinarian mode.

Stanton's eyes meet mine, then we both look back at the woman as if to say, *really?*

"You have a handful of dead students on that roof, lady," I

remind her, "so get off my ass about the only protection I have from those...*things*...out there and go do something useful."

Stanton and Macy just stare at me. It's like they don't recognize me. Then again, I hardly recognize myself. I suppose I'm genial for the most part, and pretty level headed, but after today that me is officially on hiatus.

"Go!" I shout at her, shaking her from her autocratic stance.

To her I must look unhinged. With the blood all over my face, I must look like a serial killer who escaped the mental ward and went on a killing spree getting here. Using all the brainpower she has, she complies with only a touch of hesitation.

"These freaking people," I hear myself say.

"That's Miss Titus, Mom," Macy says. "She's nice. One of the good ones."

Am I being scolded?

"Well after today, I think she should change her name to Miss Uptitus."

The joke went off like a boulder dropped in water. My attempt at gallows humor (for no reason other than I am clearly out of sorts) is not funny, even to me.

"Where to now?" I ask Stanton.

He looks at me like he's right about to ask the same question. Then: "Do I dare ask about the car?"

"I'd prefer you didn't."

He runs his hand through his hair, turns around, perplexed.

"What about your motorcycle?" I ask.

"Yeah, same," he says, suddenly stilled by the revelation.

He'd always wanted a Harley Davidson, and now something bad has happened to it. Something bad has happened to his bike like something bad happened to my brand new SUV. To this otherwise peaceful city. To the children on the school's rooftop and the children of the child development center next door.

"I have to get moving before I start crying again," I tell Stanton.

"We need to get moving before Miss Uptitus returns and gets

herself shot," he says, though his delivery is less humorous and more matter-of-fact.

For a second I wonder if he isn't working in a bit of his own gallows humor and is instead speaking the truth. Does he think I'm just going to shoot someone because I have a gun? After a second, I realize I just might, depending on how bad it gets...

CHAPTER SIX

"How can they all just cart their kids off out in the open?" Stanton asks. "Half the city is under fire and these drones... they're *still* blowing things up."

None of us say anything.

We follow the crowds of people down Page Street.

The three of us blend into the crowd making its way around the corner and up the stairs of what will soon be a large urban church. Right now it's a construction zone inside. Apparently the owner of the building was on site when the attack began, so now he's insisting the CDC and the school use his mostly gutted building as a triage center.

"Someone has to care for the injured children," he tells us when we thank him.

Like any man or woman of faith, a noble servant of God never has to tell you they are virtuous. You can see it in their actions. You can feel it in their every countenance. Like their charity comes not from an obligation to the church or even a good deed done in God's name, but from their heart because they find joy in the very act of serving others.

This is that man.

We don't even know his name; then again, names don't seem to matter much when you're in this kind of a situation. I step in and help where I can, and it takes my mind off the fear of what's happening.

Well, sort of.

The dying city still rumbles at our feet and parents continue to ask each other and Stanton if they are safe in the church since it is not yet a place of God but a work in progress.

"Whomever targeted the school and the children's center for attack isn't going to care if they blow up a church or kill more kids," I hear Macy say.

Okay, so she can sometimes be blunt.

We work the afternoon away, still fearing we'll be shot or blown up, but knowing that statistically there are almost nine hundred thousand souls living in this city. How many thousands of lives can a few hundred drones take at once?

Naturally, being an ER nurse, I'm at home in the midst of the injured. There aren't as many people to care for compared to having an entire hospital's worth of patients, but seeing all these hurt kids cuts me to the bone. To think some of them need to be rushed to the nearest hospital, but might not make it, breaks my heart.

"Who would do such a thing?" someone asks, clearly beside herself.

No one has an answer. They don't have answers like this place doesn't have bathrooms. Twice I head to the porta-potty out front and twice I can say I should've held it. Sitting on that hard plastic bowl just knowing what's marinating below turns my stomach. With my jeans circled around my ankles, I think about all the burgers, the hot dogs, the tacos, the sub sandwiches and the sodas that've gone into creating that awful smell, and honestly, when I come out (barely alive) I realize I'll never look at construction workers the same again.

As much as I'd never want someone hurt, dealing with blood

and pandemonium is worlds easier than suffering another street-side crapper.

But I'm digressing...

After hours of taking care of these kids, of watching Stanton and Macy help the building's owner devote himself fully to the tasks at hand, we're done. Everyone's been treated and given water and whatever food can be scraped up and distributed. By now, one would think the attack on the city would have stopped, or at least slowed. They'd be wrong. I can't even imagine how much damage San Francisco has endured by now.

I put that thought out of my mind, try compartmentalizing this situation the same way I compartmentalize all the drama at work.

People come and go, looking for a place to hide from the drones. A few remain, but they won't last long. Like us, they'll try to get home. What is beautiful in this tragedy, however, is how the owner never wavers in his devotion to the community. He provides food and water, offers shelter to the survivors, blesses more than a few poor souls when what they seemed to need most are the kind words of a stranger.

As the last of the parents disappear on foot, the three of us stand at the top of the concrete steps overlooking the carnage wondering if these people have any idea what's in store for them.

Hopefully the attacks will end soon.

Judging by the thick pall of smoke and the concussion bursts still hitting deeper in the city, I wonder if there's even an end in sight.

"Who do *you* think is doing this?" the owner of the building asks. None of us heard him arrive. Fortunately, we're all too tired to startle.

Stanton turns and says, "Hard to say. I know some people who might know what's going on, but I can't seem to hold a decent signal, and no one I know is answering their phones when my calls manage to ring through."

"My internet is down, too," he says. "I have friends all over town and they say the same thing. UAV's, but no idea who's controlling them."

"UAV's?" I ask.

"Unmanned Aerial Vehicles. Drones. And lots of them. They seem to be ranging anywhere from the size of a normal drone like you'd get at Best Buy to ones almost the size of a small fighter jet."

"Does anyone know anything?" Macy asks.

Some of the color has come back to her face, but it's only temporary. There are moments when she thinks about her friends and what happened to Trevor and she gets very quiet and teary eyed. Other moments, like these, she almost seems ignorant to it. I'd tell her it's okay to cry, but I think if I said that, I might break down first, and I can't do that.

Perhaps she's like Stanton and me, old enough and wise enough to tell herself to wait for safety before coming apart.

"Do you have somewhere to go?" the man asks us.

"Home," Stanton says. He doesn't even think about it. The answer just comes out and I like where his head's at.

"I hope it's still standing after today," the saint replies. Offering his hand to Stanton, the men shake hands. Turning to me, he says, "You are a gift from God, young lady." He gives me a hug and what I feel from him is a graciousness and an appreciation you just don't get from normal people.

"And you are a good Christian," I tell him with a warm smile. "Thank you so much for all you've done, for who you are."

It's time to go.

When we leave, as we start in the direction of home, I wonder what Stanton's plans are for us getting there safely.

"So the Land Rover," he says, a desperate look in his eye, "you alluded to it earlier. Is it even drivable?"

My heart sinks. I hope that's not his plan.

"The Land Rover was blown up by one of those things."

"What?" Macy asks.

"What about your motorcycle?" I ask.

"One of those UAV's—"

"Drones," Macy interjects.

"One of those drones," Stanton says, not skipping a beat, "blew up a twenty story apartment building that nearly came down on me. The dust ruined my suit, my eyes and my lungs. Somehow in the process of being dust-blind, I managed to hit a car. So no, at this point, it's not drivable."

"So what was your big plan for getting us home then?" I ask, trying not to sound manic and neurotic at the same time. I'm tired though, so I can't really help it.

"My big plan was to ask you about *your* big plan," he says, totally serious.

"You're no help at all," I grumble.

All the aches and pains of playing Smashup Derby are coming back at a relentless pace. Without a distraction, without the life-and-death situations earlier to subjugate my mind, I'm starting to realize how dire our situation really is. Well, for the moment. I don't want to sound like a drama queen or anything, but the idea of not being in my own bed tonight is beyond tragic.

"Can't we just catch a cab?" Macy asks.

Me and Stanton forgive her of her ignorance. She's just fifteen. Her friend died in her lap and we've been treating a bunch of injured kids. She's seen third degree burns, lacerated faces and limbs, crushed bones. No one really goes through that without residual effects.

"What kind of cab is going to tackle this kind of traffic," Stanton asks, his own weariness showing.

All around us, traffic has come to a stop and cars are all but abandoned. Not because people felt the need to run, but because buildings toppled both in their own footprint and sideways, blocking roadways and cars and killing pedestrians. They ran because the drones were targeting cars, and the force of the missile's impact kept vomiting out the burning bodies of its drivers and passengers for everyone to see. People didn't just leave their cars because they felt it was the best alternative, they left before they became the drones' next target.

Now that the attacks in this area have seemingly stalled, some of these brave San Franciscans are back collecting their possessions. A few are even trying to get their cars out of traffic and parked along the road. None of these attempts last long.

Unless you have a motorcycle, you aren't getting anywhere in this city.

"How far of a walk is it home?" Macy asks.

"Through this mess?" Stanton says. "Distance doesn't matter if we're under attack."

I'm looking down at Macy's shoes and thinking that as bone tired as I am, as exhausted as all of us are, who knows what the night will bring? On the plus side, back at the church we were able to wipe away some of the grime of the day, so at least we don't look like flesh eating zombies from the apocalypse. That's when we hear a faint whirring sound.

Dread overtakes me.

"Hide!" I hiss, and we all nearly freak out because at this point we're on Masonic crossing over the Panhandle. For the non-natives, the Panhandle is a long strip of grass and a few scattered trees that sit like a thin rectangular thatch of park off the main Golden Gate Park.

In other words, we're sitting ducks.

So yeah, Oak and Masonic might as well be a killing field if we don't do something quick. Macy turns and runs straight to what looks like a low-bottomed Christmas tree that's hearty with dark green needles sitting so low to the ground you have to almost crawl on hands and knees to get under it. So we do. She goes first, then me, and finally Stanton. We wiggle our way up into it. It's not pretty. These same soft needles are now pricking our skin, but it's the branches that hurt the most. They're scratching up our faces and our arms, and at this point I'm hesitant to think about all the bugs and spiders crawling around.

Naturally, my mind goes to Stanton.

He's a neat freak.

So consumed with being clean it's an old obsession I once suggested he seek therapy for. He did. His nervousness has tapered down, but his reaction to being dirty is still an anxiety with teeth. First it was the fires. Then it was the smoke and his ruined suit. Now this. He has to be going out of his mind right about now.

"You okay?" I ask.

Something blows up and we all cringe.

Giant drones are targeting the homes all along Oak Street, turning it into a shooting gallery. Fortunately we remain untouched, but I can't stop thinking of all the people who took refuge in those homes, all those people who are now homeless, injured or dead.

Like a bunch of contortionists, we hide in that tree for a good thirty minutes until the explosions finally stop. When we drop down to our hands and knees and army-crawl out, there's a weighted stillness that hangs in the smoke-filled air. Buildings are burning and people are stumbling around in the streets, not sure what to do, where to go. They're burnt, dazed and sobbing. They're plopped down on the curbs, talking to themselves, just standing there with that unblinking, thousand yard stare.

There isn't an ambulance or police responder in sight, but in the air, the uncomfortable hush that's befallen us is a weighted emptiness that feels beyond eerie. This is what the old battlefields must have felt like after the enemy had retreated and only the dead and the victorious remained.

"How much more of this can the city withstand?" I hear myself ask.

"Forget about the city for a second," Stanton says, brushing the needles from his hair and shoulder. "How much more of this can *we* withstand?"

Macy is in shock. She's wiping dirt and grass off the knees of
her white tights. She's got that look like she's thinking of Trevor
again and it's starting to twist up her face.

Did Stanton really think this was all over after we left that
church? That all we had to do was just walk home, slip into bed
and call it a day? Was I thinking that? Hoping for that?

Not me. I'm really not that naïve.

Then again, neither is he.

"We can't go home in the dark, Stanton," I tell him. "We'll
freeze before we make it. Or be killed."

The falling temperatures usher in the cold, and the cool,
damp air is pressing the acrid smells of the neighborhood deep
into the city. Our noses burn. Our eyes are rimmed red and
constantly watering.

"There are cars everywhere," Macy says.

"I know, honey," I say.

"It's not an observation, Mom. It's a suggestion. We can sleep
in one."

"Great idea," Stanton says, thrilled (in an irritated sort of
way) to finally have some reasonable input.

The three of us scout out cars, trying the doors of those vehicles we're certain aren't going anywhere. Most of the cars are
abandoned, their doors locked. Then we find a van with the
engine running, the passenger window shot out. It's a Honda
Odyssey with tinted back windows and plenty of space for three.

We didn't see the problem right away because we came up on
it from behind. Inside in the driver's seat, however, is a woman,
her body riddled with bullets, her eyes lifeless and open, staring
into another world. Outer space, perhaps.

Macy cuts between us, pulls the door open and drags the
woman out like she's an old piece of luggage. Stanton and I step
back, aghast. Maybe it was her lack of respect for the dead that
shocked us. Maybe it was just that she was doing what neither of
us could. To our absolute horror, she shoves the woman under

the van, then stands up, wipes blood from her hands on her skirt and says, "It's got gas and heat. So I opt we stay here."

"Why didn't you just kick her while you were at it?" Stanton asks without a trace of humor.

"Maybe next time," she replies.

So I guess she's not so naïve for fifteen after all.

CHAPTER SEVEN

We're able to fall asleep, but not stay asleep. The attacks seem to have stopped, but sleeping in someone's van isn't the same thing as sleeping in my bed and my body is officially protesting. We're all sleeping off and on, adjusting ourselves, readjusting ourselves, and then sitting up and trying not to cry, or scream.

"This is a nightmare," I whisper to Stanton when we both happen to be awake enough to fidget and groan at the same time. That's when the engine sputters out.

"Out of gas," Macy grumbles.

No kidding.

"What time is it?" I ask.

Stanton checks his watch and says, "Three-thirty."

"It's gonna get cold," I tell him.

"It's already cold."

The temperature didn't just drop, it plummeted. By five a.m. we were huddled together, our teeth chattering, trying to gather enough body warmth between us to ward off an impossible chill.

We manage a few more hours of sleep until we're pulled from our slumber by the far away declarations of buildings exploding and the super close sounds of glass breaking. Groggy, ill-tempered and feeling a hundred years old, I'm ready to bite people's heads off.

Reign it in, Sin, I tell myself.

Sitting up, I rub my eyes and yawn, feel my sore body opposing even that.

More glass breaking followed by the sounds of laughter. Great. In the distance, the *thunk, thunk, thunk* of this morning's bombing gathers steam and I want to cry thinking I can't take another day of this.

"Sweet Jesus," Stanton grouses.

That's when I see them. Four guys who look like gang bangers busting out car windows with shotgun stocks. They're going through gloveboxes and center consoles, pulling everything out, looking for something useful.

"We have to go," I say, but it's too late. There's already someone popping his head in the window. A fifth man. Maybe the scout.

"Awe...it's a Motel 6 on wheels," the guy says with a creepy, suggestive grin.

The gun is on the floor by my waist, but I can't get to it without being too obvious. At this point I must look like death crusted over and for that I'm grateful. As a woman being confronted by a man with bad intentions, a shotgun in hand and in the middle of doing no good, the first thing to pop into one's mind is *I'm either going to be killed or raped.*

He pulls his head back out of the passenger side window, looks up the street and whistles to his friends. It's a shrill, piercing sound. That's when I grab the gun and wait for him to stick his stupid head back in the window. It takes all of five seconds.

Pointing the weapon at him I say, "This Motel 6 isn't for you, so I suggest your move on."

He looks amused by my stance. Grinning, his expression full of mocking, he holds my eye until he decides I'm serious. The way I can be, how my DNA defines the translation of my emotions onto my face, my fear can look a lot like rage.

"My shotgun is bigger than your Glock," he says.

"It's a Sig Sauer, and I'm pretty sure I can put one right between your eyes before you even have that thing pointed in the right direction."

He puts up a hand, "Alright, alright lady. Jeez."

Backing up, he takes aim at the car and pumps a round into the side of the van. Pellets blast through sheet metal and upholstery, but fortunately it isn't where all of us are. He shot the passenger door, then laughed as he joined his friends. If he wanted to think he got one over on us, fine, I can live with that so long as he goes away.

As all of us are sitting here in the van freezing, listening to the far away symphony of destruction taking place in the direction of our home, I'm thinking about that kid. That disgusting thug and his disgusting sneer. For a second, I'm not sure if I want to deal with problems on the ground or problems in the sky.

"He shot the car, Mom."

"Thanks for keeping me up on current events," I answer in a clipped voice.

"He just shot our car and no one came out to see what happened," Macy says. "Don't you think that's strange?"

"Everyone's scared," Stanton says.

Well, duh.

"Do you hear any sirens?" she asks. Stanton shakes his head, his eyes showing signs of life.

"Is your phone working?" I ask Stanton.

"Yeah."

"Can you get an internet connection?"

He plays with it for a bit, then says, "No. What about yours?"

"Screen's cracked. Even if I can get a connection, I won't be able to see much of what I'm connected to. What about you Macy?"

She's somewhere else in her head. It's like some switch just flipped and suddenly she's gone Helen Keller. You know, deaf and mute. It's super insensitive to think like this, but I'm sorry if my PC is lacking. We're really in it here.

Looking at her, seeing her face devoid of any pure emotion, I can't even imagine what's going through her head and heart right now.

Sometime in the middle of the night, I woke to the sniffling sounds of her crying. I held her in my arms, grateful for her warmth, but more grateful that she was still alive.

"He couldn't breathe, Mom," she'd said. "It's like he was dying, but taking a long time to do it and there wasn't anything I could do for him."

"He was lucky to have you there with him when he went," I told her. I'd felt her nodding in the dark.

"Do you think I should've gone for help? Could I have saved him?"

"No, sweetheart, you couldn't have saved him."

"I should have tried, though."

"If you would've left him to go get help, he would've died alone. But because you stayed, he didn't have to. You did the right thing."

She cried herself back to sleep, and so did I.

Where Macy's pain was derived from loss, mine sprung from fear. You want so badly to protect those you love most, but when you can't, fear can darken into something worse, squeezing from your heart a flood of tears. I felt like I'd been holding back ever since this thing began, so releasing them—even in some dead woman's van in the middle of the night—was the thing my body needed most.

Now a new day is upon us, albeit one with a crappy start. My only prayer is that by day's end we'll be home, alive and still together.

"Mom," Macy says, her sad memories shelved for the moment, "I'm hungry."

I look at Stanton and Stanton looks at me, and then he looks at her and says, "Well, you'd best get used to that feeling because it might be awhile before we eat."

CHAPTER EIGHT

We get an early start. Well, as early of a start as we can after waiting for those creeps to finish breaking into all the cars up Masonic and leave. It's still cold outside and Macy is in a skirt with dirty white tights and she can't stop her teeth from chattering.

She's already wearing Stanton's suit jacket, but it's doing her no good from the waist down. Before we leave, she gets out of the van (ignoring Stanton's orders for her not to), drags the dead lady out from underneath it and starts pulling off her fuchsia colored pants. The lady is as stiff as a board, so it's not that tough a task.

Stanton looks at me and mouths the words, "What the hell?"

I shake my head in silence.

When she puts them on they're a bit too long, but not too big around the waist. She rolls the cuffs tight enough to hold, then looks up and smiles.

"Those are hideous looking," Stanton says.

I won't lie, they are.

"I'm not exactly making a fashion statement, Dad. You know that saying, 'Necessity is the mother of bad fashion?'"

"That's not a saying."

"Well it is now," she says with a quick curtsy.

"In marketing, the color fuchsia is rarely ever seen, do you know why?"

"No," Macy says with a manufactured frown, "but I'm practically bursting at the seams with curiosity."

"Because it's the one color that makes people angry."

"I'll get rid of them as soon as I can."

"Well that's a relief," he says, performing a return curtsy that gets both of them laughing.

"Can we maybe do this later," I ask. "Like when it doesn't sound like World War III a few blocks over? Those things could come back at any moment."

"UAV's," Macy says.

"Drones," Stanton replies.

"Aerial assassination squads," I say as we start walking.

"Mom's is best," Macy says.

"Yeah," Stanton agrees. "Aerial assassination squads."

The drones do come back, but it's more like they're passing by, heading to a destination that isn't us. We hide anyway. We duck into someone's stoop and we wait. We don't even care if anyone is home, that's how untenable this situation is.

From what we can see, most everyone who was out in the open when the drones attacked has either been killed, collateral damaged, or pushed one step closer to crazy town.

So we play it safe.

Extra safe.

"Should we look and see if we can find something to eat in the cars?" I ask, talking low in case the people who own the home are here.

"You must be reading my mind," Macy says.

This is the third time I've heard her stomach growl and it's so loud it's practically deafening. Or is that my own stomach? Who can really tell anymore?

We're all starving.

"Those clowns probably already found all the food," Stanton tells us.

"Maybe they weren't hungry," Macy replies. "Maybe they were looking for guns or drugs or condoms for their underage hookers."

"Don't talk like that," I say.

"It's true," Macy says. "Janine says the Mission Street gangs are pimping out twelve year olds to old geezers with blue pills and wads of cash."

"Stop with the details," Stanton says, waving his hand like he's had enough. "Besides, that's a bunch of crap and you know it."

"Is it?" she challenges.

"It is," I say, regretting that I'm even entertaining this conversation. "The real money is in the drugs."

That's when the door opens and an old man with a dusty pistol says, "Get off my porch."

We all look up at once. Stanton says, "We're sorry. It's just—"

"I know what it is," he says, cocking the hammer but not looking terribly scary doing it.

I think about showing him my gun, but Macy says, "My mom has one of those, too, but hers is bigger, nicer." She says this and then she just stares up at him, smiling.

"What did I tell you about talking to others?" Stanton says.

"Respect my elders."

"So is that any way to talk to this nice man? We're on his porch after all. Technically we're trespassing."

"I was just telling him Mom's gun is bigger and she's clearly not afraid to use it."

Shaking his head, Stanton looks up at the man and says, "I'm sorry, sir. We'll leave."

"I'm sure it's safe," he says, some of the intensity gone from his watery hound dog eyes. "Well, safe enough anyway."

"Do you have anything to eat?" Macy asks.

"I do."

After a long bout of very uncomfortable silence, Macy says, "Are you waiting for my stomach to ask you? Because it's been talking all morning."

"Wait here," he says, shutting the door. He comes back out with a granola bar and Macy is finally acting like a lady.

"That's very kind of you," she says, sugary sweet. "Thank you."

He nods, starts working his gums like he's a cow chewing his cud, then says, "You need to go now. Don't want you attracting them to my house."

We vacate the porch, but only when Macy's gobbled down half the bar does she think to ask us if we're hungry.

"Of course we're hungry, dummy," I say, and she reluctantly splits the rest of the bar in half, handing me and Stanton our respective pieces.

"We need to move faster," Stanton says, chewing his bar. "There's no cover here."

He's right, of course. You only have to insert your entire body up the tailpipe of a Christmas tree once to learn *that* lesson.

Masonic is starting to look like a poor choice of roads to travel.

On the left, it's all houses that are built so close together you can't wedge a slip of paper between them. On the right there's an elevated parking lot with a beautifully painted, waist-high wall depicting people and activity. It's all bright colors, ethnic and racial diversity, and a message of the unification of people. I love it already, but it's not going to offer us anything in the way of safety if we're attacked again.

We come up on Grove Street and nearly startle ourselves to death as we look left at a hefty man holding the biggest machine gun I've ever seen.

He sees us and puts it down immediately.

"Sorry 'bout that ladies," he says. He's got his pickup truck parked on the sidewalk and he's standing in the bed with enough fire power to turn us all into Swiss cheese. The truck is old, a white and red Chevy that's seen better days about a hundred years ago and is now just a running heap on balding tires. "Can't be too careful right now."

"That's for sure," Stanton says.

The man pulls off his hat (which says "I survived Fallujah!"), rubs a buzz cut head, then slides it back on with a slight adjustment.

"Iraq?" Stanton says.

"What gave it away?" he laughs.

Although I'm not mad at the man for finding humor in anything, perhaps he can laugh because he hasn't see what we've seen, or survived what we just did. But then again, if he was in Fallujah, from what I know about that hell hole, it would seem we've seen nothing the likes of which he's seen, suffered and survived.

"Thank you for your service," I find myself saying to him.

"You're quite welcome." Pointing down, he says, "Whatcha got in your pants there?"

"Sig Sauer," I tell him.

"What caliber you using?" he says. I shrug my shoulders. "You even fired it yet?"

"She took it off a dead cop," Macy says, which earns her a stern look from Stanton. "What? It's true?"

"Can I take a look?"

"Will you give it back?" I ask him.

"Do I look like I'm starving for weapons over here?" he asks. Taking a few steps toward him, I take a peek inside the bed of his truck and it looks like the mother of all armories.

"I guess not," I say, handing him the weapon.

He ejects a round, looks at it then nods his head. He then sights a tree and fires the weapon making me and Macy jump. Stanton doesn't even budge.

"So he's been around weapons before, but you two haven't."

I nod. His father grew up on a farm.

The stranger clicks on the safety, tosses the gun to Stanton who catches it. He then leans down and tosses him a big box of ammo. It says Elite Performance and shows some up-close pictures of bullets on it.

"There's fifty rounds of nine millimeter in there. Won't hold off an army, but maybe if any of these Mexican turds come after you, you can put the fear of God into 'em."

"That's racist," Macy says.

"No, that's a fact. The Sureños and the Norteños are loosely related to the Latino gangs of the same name from the late 1960's. Latino is Mexican. Just like my wife. Born and raised on the streets of Ciudad Juarez."

"That's not an easy place to grow up," Stanton says.

"Near impossible."

"How'd you two meet?" I ask. I'm a sucker for a good love story.

"She snuck over the border into El Paso one night with friends. We met, spent the whole night talkin' and kissin' and in the end she decided to stay."

"Do her parents know where she's gone?" Macy asks. "That she's with you?"

He laughs and there's enough warmth to it to know he's a good man. "Her father was beheaded and left for dead in the middle of an intersection and her mother was running drugs for the cartel to make ends meet. Being here is better for her. Telling her mom was her choice, but that didn't make it easy."

"How long have you been married?"

"Four years next week," he says, his eyes still moving, still assessing the streets around us. "Assuming there is a next week."

"Why are you out here?" Stanton asks. "Shouldn't you be inside keeping her safe?"

"See that building back there?" he says, hitching a thumb over his shoulder.

All we see is the tall brick building we're standing in front of and a city road with a slight grade and one blown up car that's now just a charred skeleton on melted wheels.

"There are a lot of buildings," Stanton says.

"That's a city college that's set up like a fortress, even though it wasn't intended that way. It's been evacuated, so last night we moved in. Me, my Army buddies and our wives and their children. You see, it's fortified. Me being out here is me keeping her safe. Got a buddy up at the end of the street doin' the same. We served together."

"The college is a big target," I say.

Sitting down on an old, turned-over milk crate inside the bed of his truck, he says, "Yeah, but it's also an empty target if you're thinking like the enemy. See, the drones don't want big targets, they want catastrophic loss of life if you're following the patterns. Now that everyone's running home, they're targeting the homes, not so much the buildings where people *used* to be."

"So you're out here..." I say, letting the statement hang.

"Watching out for gang bangers and keeping the skies clear in case the MQ-1's start sniffing around, or heaven forbid, the RQ-1's."

"What are the...MQ—"

"Predator drones. The MQ-1's are aerial reconnaissance. Strictly observe and report. The RQ-1's are tactical. Well, so are the MQ-1A's if you want to get technical."

"We don't," Macy says.

He gives a hearty laugh, then says, "They're basically the big drones with the big missiles that are hitting everything. Those are Hellfire missiles that were first designed for anti-tank applications. They're no joke."

"So the government's doing this?" Macy asks.

"No," he says. Looking at me, he says, "I like this little firecracker."

"So do we, most times."

"Who do *you* think is behind these attacks?" Stanton asks.

Just then the former soldier with the stolen Mexican wife

stands up, fully alert, and stares straight ahead. We turn and see a threesome of thugs walking down Grove toward us. He puts up his machine gun and they stop and show us their pistols.

Moving so fast I can't hardly comprehend the speed, the man has the barrel flipped over, the butt of the weapon in his armpit and his sights set on the incoming trio.

They all flip him the bird until he puts a round right at their feet. They turn and run and he says, "Pretty soon they'll be back with their friends. You don't want to be here when that happens. Oh, and don't go down there. Not unless you want your daughter becoming one of their—"

"Underage hookers?" Macy says.

"I, uh..."

"Told you, Dad," she grins.

"Teach her to shoot when you can," our new friend says, sitting back down on his old red crate. "That's what the box of ammo is all about."

"What if this is over in the next few days?"

"It ain't gonna be," he says, nonchalant. "It ain't gonna be over for awhile."

"Why do you say that?" I ask.

"That's not the government flying them drones. I'm pretty sure it's the *drones* flying them drones. This is Artificial Intelligence. AI. It's 2017 all over again, but this time those morons in Palo Alto have no way to shut them down. Not unless they set off an EMP, but that'd have to be nuclear and you can damn sure bet they won't be doing that anytime soon."

"What's a nuclear EMP?" I ask.

"Electromagnetic Pulse. Nuclear suggests it's high altitude, the higher the better. Eighty thousand feet is ideal if you want the widest coverage. A blast like that basically shuts down anything with electronics in it, including the electrical grid. If the charge is enough, if this isn't an isolated incident—and I suspect it isn't—then two of these nuclear EMP's can shut down the entire country. Considering the National Guard ain't here, and the Air Force ain't here, I'm thinking we're going to be in it real quick. And a lot worse than this. But I'm a man of war, and paranoia is my drug of choice so maybe I've just seen too much combat."

"Either way, you're saying we're pretty much on our own right now," Stanton says, swallowing what looks like a hulking lump in his throat.

"Indeed. Unless you want to bunk with us."

"That's very nice of you," I say, "but we're headed home."

"Where's home?" he asks, his eyes alert.

"850 Powell Street, just off Sacramento Street across from The Fairmont in the Financial District."

He whistles like he knows the place, like he knows how nice it is. Suddenly I'm self-conscious of where we live and scared I sound pompous when I'm anything but that.

"Nice digs over there. Real nice digs. Well, they were nice, but now they're not. Probably just rubble by now."

"You can't know that," I say.

The guy leans forward, grabs something, then comes up with a huge pair of binoculars and says to Stanton, "Get up here, see for yourself."

He obliges the man, looks in the direction of our home, then returns the field glasses. His face is bloodless, his expression clearly that of someone shaken by what they've seen.

"Stanton?" I ask.

He climbs off the truck, thanks the man, then looks at me and Macy and says, "We should leave him to his post."

"You have a place to stay if yours ain't around," the man calls after us.

"What's your name?" Macy asks.

"Waylon."

"Nice to meet you, Waylon," she says.

Macy and I wave, and Stanton thanks him for the ammo, but judging by the way my husband is moving, there is a pretty good chance he's thinking our home is no longer standing.

CHAPTER NINE

We make our way up Masonic, trudging along the sidewalk like a pack of derelicts. At Fulton Street, Stanton decides to keep going straight. Where is he going?! Is he just walking for the sake of walking, or is he actually thinking? Or clearing his head? Perhaps he's pondering the meaning of life now that it appears human life is being stamped out by rogue technology.

"Do you have a destination, Stanton, or are we just getting in our ten thousand steps?"

"No," Stanton says. "And yes."

He keeps moving.

"Then why are we even walking?" Macy asks. "Because my legs hurt, my back hurts, I'm tired and that granola bar didn't do squat but make me more hungry."

Stanton stops and turns to face us both. Half manic, he says, "We need a place to stay. We need water, food and shelter, so if anyone has a suggestion, I'm open to it."

"You look insane," Macy says.

"Maybe I am!"

"So that's it then?" Macy grumbles. "We're going to be squatters?"

Stanton starts walking again.

"What did you see?" I ask. "Is our home there or not?"

He doesn't say anything. He just keeps walking, so I stop asking questions. Behind me Macy's shoes are slapping the sidewalk in protest. There's a bit of an incline past Fulton, but it feels more like we're walking up the side of a mountain as tired as we are.

"Do you want to sleep in a car again?" I ask her.

"As long as no one died in it, at this point, I don't care. Then again, if it's a comfortable car, I don't care if five people died in it."

"That's morbid," Stanton grumbles.

"This whole situation is morbid," I tell him. After awhile, to my kind, loving, patient husband (I hope you're catching my sarcasm at this point), I ask, "Do you ever think things will be normal again?"

"Are you looking in these people's eyes?" he says, a long, sharp edge to his words. "Half of them look like they're in shock, like their brains just melted out of their ears the moment all their precious things were destroyed."

"I feel like that," I say, my voice rising. "I feel like that and you're not telling me if all our precious things are destroyed." Rushing up to him, I grab his arm, haul him around. "Are our things destroyed?"

He shakes off my arm and says, "I don't know!"

"Stop!" Macy screams.

We all stand together, huffing and puffing, nostrils flared, ready to kill each other, unable to understand each other.

"Are we homeless, Stanton?" I ask, softer now, my vision blurring behind the threat of tears.

"I...I think...I don't know. But if we can't make it home today, I can't sleep in another car someone's died in. I'm just not doing it."

Macy folds her arms, looks away.

In the distance, the smoke is billowing again, turning the skies gray. All around us, flakes of ash are falling like the first winter's snow. We almost don't even notice, but then it's hard not to. Glancing around, seeing people mill about, watching them walking aimlessly, absent-mindedly, like they're complete freaking space cadets, I wonder if this is our end.

"I'm scared, Stanton," I say, feeling a tear skim my cheek. Wiping it quickly, dragging a finger under my other eye to mop up the puddling of more tears, I say, "Aren't you?"

Speaking low under his breath, he says, "I feel broken, Sin. It makes me feel weak."

"You're not weak," I whisper back, taking a step towards my husband, the father of my child, my soul mate.

He falls into silence.

As his wife of sixteen years, I know this stillness in him. I know exactly what it means. It means that behind that teetering façade there's a strong, competent man losing his grip on life. He can handle almost anything, but force him to consider his mortality and he becomes this sweet, fragile thing. Another step forward and I'm in his arms. Holding him. Trying not to cry on his shoulder because his shoulder smells like the downfall of civilization.

"I don't know what to do, Sin. For the first time in my life, I'm truly at a loss."

"Me too, baby. We need to figure this out though. If we don't...if we don't we'll die. Macy will die."

His body stiffens and I can tell he's biting back the tears. Seconds later another set of arms curls around us both and I feel Macy hugging us and this about breaks my heart.

"Two days ago I would have been so embarrassed about this, but now I could care less," she says. Stanton and I can't help laughing. "I love you guys. Thank you for coming to get me."

Moving out of my arms into hers, he pulls her close, kisses the top of her head and says, "I might not have if I knew you were going to wear those butt-ugly pants."

Now we're all laughing, and maybe crying, but the moment

isn't long because we hear the sounds of explosions getting closer.

My eyes find Macy's face. She's wiping her eyes, the light of joy leaving them dim once more. She's quite a sight. The cuffed fuchsia pants underneath the black skirt with the non matching red sweater and the black (now grey) platforms, my eyes go to the collar of her white blouse (how it's half smoked and half spattered with Trevor's blood) and I'm overwhelmed with sadness. She needs to change her shirt, get into something that doesn't remind us that her friend didn't make it.

"We have to go," Stanton says. "We need to find a place to stay. Maybe a vacant building or something."

"If we find a house, honest to God," I hear myself saying, "I'm taking the longest, hottest shower ever."

"I just want something to drink," Macy says. "My mouth is like the desert right now. I can practically use my saliva as chewing gum."

"That's gross," Stanton says.

"I'm not exactly camera ready," she replies.

We're walking up Masonic Street having gone God knows how many blocks uphill and I can't stop feeling we're not getting any closer to where we need to go. Which is a house. There are tons to choose from, but not on this street, so I'm not sure what the deal is.

"Are you headed to a neighborhood?" I ask. "Because we're passing up a lot of beautiful homes."

"I know you want a house, but the bullets guy, back in the truck, he said people are better off in buildings rather than homes."

"It's because the machines expect them to be empty," Macy says, still dragging her feet, "so that makes them safe."

"You have to get past the idea that anything's safe, honey," I say. "At least for now."

We're coming upon an intersection full of abandoned cars. There are normal people rooting through them now. Not people who look like deviants or gang bangers. Should we be going through them, too? We have a weapon, but no food, no water, no shelter. Suddenly I'm feeling very vulnerable.

An anxiety is arising in me, one I have to force down.

It's when we hear some of these cars still running that we put two and two together. Inside these cars are dead people, shot-to-death-by-drones people.

Logically we know these are the best cars to search because nothing was taken from them (yet). You just have to hope the doors are open, unless you have something solid enough to break the glass. We do. Stanton has the butt end of the pistol.

We go to work on this Honda Accord, breaking the glass on the second try. Someone nearby says, "Hey, have some respect!"

Stanton and I fall into a moment's pause as we eye this woman with two bottles of water half stuffed in her pockets. Macy doesn't skip a beat, though. She opens the door from the inside, drags the driver out (it's a twenty-something kid with a scraggly beard and a man bun) then steps over him and gets into the car.

If only the Accord wasn't packed in between a bunch of other cars, all three of us could have climbed in, buckled up and fled the scene. But this is just wishful thinking right now.

The woman with the bottled water stands there fixated on Macy, her jaw hanging slack, disbelief coloring her eyes all shades of red. "Have you no respect for the dead?" she barks.

"I have more respect for life than death at this point," Stanton calls out. "Now go back to your own cars before we shoot you in the face and take your water."

Mortified, she abandons the hunt altogether, stomping up the street in a huff, muttering things that sound like an argument, then turning and screaming curse words at us that we're too busy to pay attention to.

"Would you use it?" I ask Stanton when the crazy lady is gone. "The gun, I mean? Would you use it on another human?"

"Jackpot!" Macy says.

After finding nothing useful in the center console or the glovebox, she's heading for the backseat, squeezing her body in between the seats and wiggling over the center console. In back there's an old box with the flaps ripped off. Inside is a big blanket that Macy's pulling out and pressing to her face.

"It's not going to be so cold tonight ladies and germs!"

"In Darwin's world of survival of the fittest," I say, "I think we're going to be okay."

"Darwin can suck it," Macy quips, getting out of the car.

By now she's got the blanket draped around her shoulders. She's pulling it tight across her chest, telling us how warm it is.

"Maybe you should get his pants, too," Stanton says. Macy looks past us, at his pants, and says, "Too much blood on them."

This silences us. This and the whirring sounds of the drones.

For a second we all drop to our knees, ready to scurry underneath the car in case those things come after us this time.

Just ahead is Geary Street which will take us to Laurel Heights. It's not the Financial District, or a multimillion dollar condo, but the homes there are nice enough.

Scanning the air, our ears attuned to the sounds of the UAV's, I see the University of San Francisco and it looks like a bombed out ruin. To the right, just up the street is Raoul Wallenberg High School. Judging by the giant plumes of smoke billowing into the sky, it's the same story there.

Forcing myself to think of circus clowns or whatever (a beautiful steak dinner), I try not to think about all the murdered students. About how many are still in there. About their families, the ones living in other states or countries who have no idea what's happening here.

"They're gone," Stanton says, speaking about the drones.

We get to our feet then finish searching the cars. Now more than ever, I'm feeling how sticky my lips have become, how my throat is so dry not even the summoning of saliva is enough.

"We need water," I say.

Seconds later a pair of drones zoom by not fifteen feet over our heads. Macy and I duck into the backseat of a nearby Ford F-150; Stanton jumps into the front passenger seat next to a dead guy who's face down on the steering wheel, the spider-webbed windshield painted red.

When they're gone, Stanton says, "Check the glovebox."

Inside is a map of the city, a two-pack of Bic lighters and a locking lug nut for his custom wheels. I grab the lighters and the map.

"Get the lug nut," he says.

"Why?"

He rolls his eyes and I get it.

"Macy, open the driver's side door for me, please."

She gets out and does just that. Stanton gets on his butt, braces himself, then uses both feet and his leverage to shove the man over. The dead guy spills out of the car without an ounce of grace. He lands on his head, his body not quite making it out.

With his head wrenched sideways, half his face is smashed into the pavement, but his body is propped up on the truck with his legs half in the air. It's like a handstand of death, but with no hands. Macy looks away. Maybe it's his position, but maybe it's that one of his eyes was shot out.

Stanton gets out of the truck walks around and perfectly deadpan, he says, "Well that could've gone better."

He grabs a leg and begins unlacing the man's right shoe. He pulls it off, tosses it over his shoulder then peels a long beige sock off his foot.

Did I tell you I hate seeing other people's feet? I do. Most of them...they're just plain nasty. Especially this guy's. I don't even want to tell you what's up with his toenails.

"Lug nut?" he says, hand out, palm up.

I hand him the heavy silver nut and he drops it into the sock, tying the top of it into a knot.

"Stand back," he says.

We oblige him.

He swings the thing in the air and now I see it. He's made us another weapon. In case bullets don't work, we can beat people to death with this here sock.

Macy's smiling now, which makes me smile.

Turning his attention to the F-150, he stands back, swings it as hard as he can and hits the back window, shattering it.

"Holy cow!" he says, surprising us both with a look of satisfaction.

"Nice, Dad," Macy adds, and even I'm nodding my head in approval. He hands the sock to our daughter, almost like he's handing over the keys to the kingdom.

"Anyone gets out of line, swing this down on their forehead as hard as you can."

"Stanton," I say.

"What?"

"Won't this kill a person?" Macy asks, swinging it around.

"You could always go underhand and catch them in the baby maker," he says.

"Hold this?" Macy asks me.

She bequeaths me the gigantic blanket and I take it. She then walks up to the truck and starts swinging the loaded sock backwards, really getting it going. When she's got the timing down, she steps forward and shoots it at the truck where it smacks the back door with a ferocious *bang!*

"Holy crap!" she says, looking at the huge dent the nut left behind.

"Impressive," Stanton says.

And me? I'm having a hard time with my husband teaching Macy how to hurt people. Maybe I'm being too overprotective of her. Maybe Stanton's right.

A few cars up, we hit what Stanton believes is an even bigger jackpot. Macy pulls something big and green and tightly packaged out of the center console.

"What about this?" she says, holding up a brick of weed.

"I almost want to say yes," I tell her, "but given that the

bottom's fallen out of this city and we need to be on our toes, I'd say leave it."

"Are you kidding?" Stanton says. "We're taking it with us."

"Since when do you do drugs?" I ask.

"Never. But we're in gang territory, so maybe this is our get-out-of-death card."

Macy's sniffing it, then turning away and making a face.

"As much as I appreciate your logic, I'm not toting around a bunch of weed so you'd better make sure you know how to use your gun."

"I do."

"But would you?" I ask.

He knows what I'm asking. I want to know if he'll pull the trigger to protect his family.

"These are different times. Maybe they won't always be this way, but right now they are. So yes. If it comes to it, then yes."

"Are you guys talking in code?"

"Yes," we say together.

Our eyes meet and there's a resolve I trust. Slowly I'm nodding my head (*I believe you*), and he's giving me a reassuring smile (*I'll never let anything bad happen to you*).

The thing about Stanton is he works (worked) in the Transamerica pyramid inside the financial district about twenty-seven hours a day and I work (worked) in the ER just as much. We live (lived) an affluent lifestyle, but it's taken a toll on us both emotionally and physically over the years. Our home is (might be past tense, as in *was,* but the jury's still out on that one) gorgeous, worth every penny of the three million we paid for it, but now all that might be gone. All things considered—and I know it won't be easy—I'm starting to think we've got thick enough skin for this.

A second thought crawls over the first, but it sounds a lot like a warning: *whatever you're expecting this to be, it's going to be far worse than even you can imagine.*

"No on the weed," I say and Macy tosses it back in the truck.

"C'mon Macy. We're going home."

"To our home?" she asks.

"Whatever home we sleep in, shower in, eat in, *that's* our home," I say. "Got it?"

Stanton suddenly goes very rigid.

"Shhh," he hisses.

He's listening with an ear to the sky and that's when three blocks up Masonic a huge pair of drones carpet bomb the six or seven story Public Storage building, a nearby big box retailer and rows upon rows of nearby homes. Public Storage collapses onto Masonic street in a heap of smoke and powder, spilling its bricks and damaged contents out over dozens of abandoned cars.

"Let's go!" Stanton says, breaking into a run.

We follow as fast as we can, cutting down Turk Street, but the earth is shaking beneath us and the bombing raids have anyone caught outside running in doors. Someone's left a one gallon jug of water on the roof of their car in a panic; I sprint across the street to grab it and keep running.

"Cincinnati!" Stanton yells over the noise.

"Water!" I scream.

By the time I catch up, I'm out of breath and that's when a fleet of drones appears up the street. Stanton turns us into a narrow stairway leading up a hillside, a stairway that's fairly well hidden. It's made of concrete and flanked by two homes and tons of trees and foliage. For whatever reason, I think of the stairway in *The Exorcist* and this gives me a second's pause. Did I tell you I hate horror movies? Yeah. I'm a big chicken when it comes to demonic possession, serial killers, inbreeding hill people.

Sin, the drones...

I keep moving. As the three of us hustle up the stairs, my legs feel more destroyed than ever and I swear to God, my lungs are on fire. Stopping means dying though, and this has me pushing hard. The rapid concussion sounds of dozens of bombs being dropped isn't lost on me.

The drones zip by and we all heave a collective sigh, but at the top of the stairs are two rough looking guys who are glancing down past Stanton to get a good look at me and Macy. Macy is in front of me. All I can see are those ugly pants of hers.

They aren't going to save us.

What I'm thinking at this exact moment is that we aren't unattractive women, not by any measure. I've been considering this for the last few hours. Will our slovenly condition mask our good looks, or will guys like these see through them?

I think I can handle myself, but Macy? I can't even begin to tell you how much I worry about her innocence.

Now I'm thinking of my child not from my own perspective, but from a boy's viewpoint. No, a *man's* viewpoint.

She's very cute in the face and at the age where she's no longer too young for the consideration of older boys and younger twenty-somethings. That's to say she's got her boobs and her hips are coming in, taking her from boyish straight toward the more curvy look of a woman. Honestly, she's growing up too fast. She's becoming a woman.

Considering the lawlessness we've seen so far, I'd bet my last breath this terrifies Stanton about as much as it terrifies me. Maybe more. Neither of us have spoken about this, but I can feel it in his soul as much as I'm sure he can feel it in mine.

"There are two of them," one of the guys says to the other, his tone betraying his intentions, "and two of us. We just need *him* out of the way and I think we'll have a love connection."

These guys are about five steps ahead of Stanton with the high ground; the one talking has a shotgun at his side. The other is looking over his shoulder, perhaps at the neighborhood that was almost bombed into the Stone Age.

"I think you guys can be each others' love connection," Stanton jokes, even though I can tell he's agitated, not amused.

"I'm into girls," the one toting the shotgun says. "Young girls. Blondes especially."

"Right now survival is the flavor of the day, fellas," Stanton says. "In case you hadn't heard, all that smoke in the air isn't from guys like you lighting up blunts and listening to Snoop Dogg in your grandmother's basement or whatever. There's actual death happening out there."

"Yeah?" one says to Stanton in a sick, mocking tone. Then to his buddy, he says, "About to be one more on the dead guy list, don't you think?"

Stanton draws the pistol, pulls the trigger and the guy drops. He shoots the other one before he can run, then scampers up the last few stairs in case there are more of them on the other side. Fortunately for all our sakes, there aren't. Right about now I can't breathe.

Is this really happening?

My eyes watch as my husband drags the second kid off the sidewalk, both of them moaning in pain. He grabs the shotgun, tosses it to me (which I catch on my way up the stairs) and tells Macy to look away. He waits for more bombs to drop, and when they do, he puts a single round into each of their heads.

CHAPTER TEN

Leaning over the boys' bodies, Stanton goes through their jeans (pocket knife, lighter, three shotgun shells—he crushes and discards half a pack of smokes). Every so often, glancing up at the ground-level neighborhood we popped up into, my brave, reckless husband looks perfectly poised.

This scares the absolute crap out of me.

He barely even hesitated. Who is this man that I married? He looks at me and I'm scared at what he's seeing in my eyes. He returns to the bodies.

"You didn't even give them a chance," I all but whisper.

Without looking up, he says, "You heard what they said, right? Didn't you see what I saw? How they were looking at you and Macy? And that one idiot saying he likes young girls...that was reason enough."

"That's not proof they're rapists," I say.

"Not now maybe," he says. "But guys like these are opportunists, and today there are more than enough opportunities. You two won't be theirs. And neither will I."

I find myself pacing in a tight line.

He just killed them.

Stopping, looking down at them, I can't believe they were

breathing a moment ago, and now they're not. How is Stanton not freaking out?

How am *I* not freaking out?

Macy comes up behind me, takes the water jug out of my hand and drinks. "Not too fast," I say.

She lets up, burps, then says, "Man I needed that!"

I drink a bit myself, then hand it to Stanton who waves it off because he's busy. I take another sip, hand it to Macy and tell her to ration it.

She knows exactly what I mean.

Looking everywhere else, not even flinching as things explode a few blocks away, I see a neighborhood that looks relatively untouched by the chaos.

"This is nice," I hear myself say. "The houses here."

I turn around and see Macy looking down at the two boys. Stanton is standing up. He's got another shotgun shell that he's stuffing into his pocket. I hand him the water. He drinks, slowly. It's just several sips while he's looking around. His eyes are roving—going to windows, cars, potential hiding places.

After he decides we're not in imminent danger, he relaxes his eyes, his demeanor.

"It is nice," he says. He adjusts the contraband in his pockets, then: "Let's see if we can find ourselves a house."

"What if there are more of them?" Macy asks.

"I don't think there are," Stanton says. "Otherwise you'd see a lookout, some other evidence of gang activity."

"You think they're gang members?" I ask.

Stanton fires me a look. Apparently, as far as he's concerned, if they carry guns and talk about having sex with young girls in front of said girl's parents...they're gang bangers. It's a stereotype, sure, but it's *his* stereotype.

Frowning, I pull Macy aside.

It's not the bullet holes or the blood that tells the story of these two knuckleheads. It's the tattoos. They're all skulls and names and numbers. They're full sleeves. The ink spanning from wrist to earlobe...on *both* arms. One of them has three tear drops tattooed under his right eye.

"It's good you shot them," Macy says, and this saddens me. Actually this crushes me inside. I thought I raised my child to have more respect for life than this.

Is she thinking of Waylon, the Iraq war vet, and what he said about the neighborhood gangs? Is Stanton? Perhaps these *were* the types of kids he was warning us about. Or perhaps we'll never know.

"You shouldn't feel like that," I tell her.

"Yes, she should," Stanton says, looking up and down the block. "You can't be this soft, Sin. Not now."

"This isn't the wild west."

He turns and snaps at me. "Look around, Cincinnati. It sure as hell is!"

"Dad," Macy says, calming him down a bit.

We step into the neighborhood, round a corner and see a trio of bodies. This is residential, so we expect to see something like this, but nothing prepares you for seeing the body of a small child.

My eyes focus on the girl.

She's wearing a pink dress and one of her white shoes had come off her foot. It has a small silver buckle. The minute I see her white tights—her little foot twisted sideways—I turn away, stifle a cry. Something in my soul cracks, breaks. The image is in me now, burned into my brain. She can't be more than three years old.

"These...animals," I say, half angry, half struggling not to have a total breakdown.

"These things are neither human nor animal, Sin," Stanton says in a wet, choked up voice. "They're machines and they have no sense of morality. No hesitation, no respect for life, no remorse."

Looking at the homes, the sounds of bombing stall out only to be replaced by a cold, steady silence. Lately we've come to distrust these subtle platitudes. We pass the little girl and a woman a few feet ahead of her. *Was this her child?* They're both sprawled face-down on the sidewalk. The woman has a meaty red mess in the crown of her head while the child has two red blooms in her back.

Ahead, propped against someone's garage door, is a handsome young man. He's got a dried red carnation over his heart. Not the flower. Blood. Judging by the rust colored smears on the sidewalk, he dragged himself over to the garage, perhaps in search of cover. Not that it provided any cover at all. His head is lolled forward, his chin sitting on his chest. On his ring finger is a shiny gold band. I look over at the two bodies. Was that woman his wife? Was that his child?

On second thought, she looks too old for him—what I can see of her. Maybe the woman was his mother and the little girl was his. Maybe they were neither. Just strangers in the wrong place at the right time.

"Do you hear that?" Stanton asks. Collectively we perk up. "I can't be sure, but...I think that might be them."

Stanton's on the move, looking for open doors because there's no decent place to hide from these things but inside a home.

The first two doors are locked.

Now we all hear are the approaching sounds of more than one UAV. Stanton kicks in the third door. It splinters, the frame cracking completely. He kicks it again and it swings in hard, bouncing back. The three of us hustle inside, slamming the door behind us as best as we can.

"Conversion," Stanton says looking around, breathing hard.

Instead of this being a single home with three stories, there's a tight staircase heading up to the second floor, then presumably another heading up to the third floor. The first door says UNIT A.

The construction isn't pretty, but it serves its purpose.

Each floor, it appears, has been renovated into its own separate home. The reason for this? Money, of course. The owner was working to milk the property for as much rent as he or she could collect.

Typical capitalists.

I grab the knob of UNIT A's door and twist. It's locked. Macy shoves by me, grabs the handle and gives it her own valiant effort. It doesn't open so she starts to shake it with all her might, her nerves finally spinning out of control.

Wow.

Ever since her school was shot up and Trevor died, she's been halfway herself. The stores of emotion are bleeding out now. They were bound to erupt somewhere.

When Macy finally gives up, Stanton says, "You had your chance."

We move out of the way.

He's rearing back to kick this door down when we hear a voice on the other side of it saying, "We're armed in here! Leave us alone or we'll...we'll shoot!"

Stanton ponders the warning, looking at us. I shrug my shoulders. He looks up the stairs, pauses. Outside, something else starts shooting.

"Get down!" he barks.

We drop to our knees and cover our heads just as a handful of bullets blast through the main door. They bury themselves into the wall where we were all just standing, which has me feeling part queasy, part relieved.

Standing back up, my eyes won't stop looking at five big, splintery holes in the door we just kicked in. Holes that have distinct rods of light spearing their way inside. It's only now that I realize I've still got the shotgun Stanton took from the dead kids by *The Exorcist* stairway.

"Upstairs," Stanton says.

We quickly creep up the stairs following on Stanton's heels as fast as humanly possible. The instant we hit the second floor landing, the door to UNIT B is pulled open and a shotgun barrel is shoved in our faces by some old lady in a fluffy pink bathrobe.

Her bloodshot eyes are flashed wide, the vessels straining against the bumpy whites of her eyes and brown irises that might have one day been chocolaty brown, but now just look like day old toast.

"This is my house *you criminals!*" Her voice is like a cast iron skillet being dragged down the sidewalk. Her look is like we're cannibals who just ate her only child.

Stanton uses a hand to move us behind him, then he raises both hands in mock surrender and says, "The drones...they're out there, shooting at people. Honest. We just need a place to duck into until they pass. We mean you no harm. I promise."

It's right then that I actually think about the way we look. How we don't look like the well dressed socialites we were just two days ago before the floor gave out on this city. Her eyes are seeing me with my shotgun, my plastic jug of water. I'm sliding the weapon around my back.

Out of sight, out of mind, right?

"Your promises and a bag of chips are worth less than a bag of chips," she says, her vocal chords strained from the outburst. Her reply wasn't so much of a slant as it was a sad state of affairs for her.

"You don't look well," Stanton says in a calm, disarming tone.

The decrepit woman's frown pulls into a telling grimace. She racks the shotgun and in that exact same moment, houses inside the neighborhood start blowing up. The structure shakes, catching us all off guard. Everyone but Stanton. He grabs the woman's shotgun barrel, ducks under it and drives it toward the ceiling.

The woman loses her grip on the rifle, her bingo arms wheeling in slow motion as she stumbles backwards toward a thick area rug in the center of the living room. Stanton rushes through the door reaching for her arm, trying to catch her, but it's too late.

Her heel catches and she tumbles tush over teakettle, cracking her head on the edge of a metal coffee table. Another run of bombing rocks the ground beneath the house, causing surface cracks to split along the walls and knock some plaster chips off the ceiling.

Looking at the old woman, blood soaking the white rug, even I know it's all done but the crying.

"Dad!" Macy says, moving around him. "You killed her!"

"If she's dead, it would have been the fall that killed her," I hear myself saying, horrified by my own go-to response despite this being the truth.

Dropping to a knee to check her head, I realize she is indeed gone. How am I supposed to rationalize this? It was an accident, right? It had to be.

Accidents happen.

Three dead people inside of twenty minutes. I look up at Stanton and he's running his hands through his hair, his eyes wild with frenzy. It's all sinking in. He can't believe this is happening.

None of us can.

Looking at the woman's skeletal frame, her exposed chicken legs, how delicate and dainty her wrists were, even a blind man can see she was on the verge of starvation. One boisterous fart and her spine would have stress fractured on its own.

Tears gather in my eyes for what I'm seeing and feeling. For what just happened.

"I did this," Stanton says, clearly stunned, his face losing color fast. "This is my fault. I...I shouldn't have—"

"Don't," I say, standing up. "This isn't on you. You tried to catch her, I saw it."

We all stand over the body in silence, our eyes glued to the old woman who's just laying there with her mouth dropped open and her head cranked sideways.

Surviving this assault on the city is not going the way we thought it would. Looking at the fissures on the wall, the splintered glass, the cracked thatch of drywall lying on the hardwood floor, we're now realizing there will be casualties of our own making. Does that make us bad people? We're not bad people. But still, they say judge a man not by his words but by the force of his deeds.

How will I judge my husband? After all, when I asked him if he could protect us, if he would, he said yes.

He said yes.

"You could see it in her," my mouth says, almost on its own. "Her will to go on was gone. She was defending her home because she needed to. Because this is where she was planning on dying and she wasn't up for the company."

"Good story, Mom," Macy says, her eyes dry but her emotions clearly unwound.

Turning around, I say, "Shut the door!"

She does.

Looking at Stanton I ask, "Are we bad people?"

His gaze won't leave the old woman's crippled frame. Tears slide into the bowl of his eyes, then roll over the lid and drip onto his cheeks.

"You're not. But I...I think that maybe...I think I am. I think that's just what happened, Sin. I think I just became a bad person."

CHAPTER ELEVEN

We're starting to realize there's something much larger at play here. "This isn't a terrorist attack," Stanton says. "It can't be."

The siege is coordinated and substantial. It seems every corner of the city is getting hammered to one degree or another. But there aren't enough drones to hit us all at once, and there weren't enough bombs to flatten the entire city in a day. That means we have a chance. It means San Francisco still has a chance.

Or is that the lie we'll tell ourselves to keep on going?

Honestly, I can't be sure.

The point is, the more destruction we see, the more our moods sink. The more we are forced to admit that if this concentrated effort to cripple our city isn't the work of terrorists looking to make a statement, it could very well be what Stanton says it is: self-governed machines working on behalf of rogue AI trying to stamp out every last human soul.

Downstairs, the unrelenting croon of a woman sobbing keeps the silence from taking hold. We're out of the woods, though. For now anyway. The old lady has a bed, clean sheets, two good blankets. She has food, cold water, some medicine.

"About that shower," I say, and no one protests.

In the bathroom I peel off my clothes, avoid my face in the mirror, then wait until the water is hot enough to step inside the old tub. Pulling the shower curtain closed reminds me of my college days, but there is nothing nostalgic about this place.

Five minutes becomes ten and I find myself sitting down, arms pulled around my knees, sobbing. There's a knock on the bathroom door I don't respond to. The door opens then closes. The drapes come back a bit but I don't look up.

"Are you okay?" Stanton asks.

I give a subtle nod. I don't hear the curtain close, but when the door opens then closes, I go back to crying.

Twenty minutes later I'm blow drying my hair, looking at myself in the small mirror but not really looking much. My eyes look tired. I feel depleted.

When I walk into the living room, which is now all hard-wood floors, an old couch, the coffee table and a flat panel TV, Macy says, "Did you save any hot water?"

"I think. Where's your father?"

"He rolled the old lady up in the carpet, then said he was going to...I don't know, do something with her."

"Like chuck her in a nearby dumpster?" I hear myself saying.

Me and Macy look at each other, neither of us blinking. "I don't think he wanted to kill those boys," Macy says. "I think it's starting to bother him."

"It would concern me if it *didn't* bother him. Especially the old lady."

"Yeah," she says, reflecting.

"Did he find a shovel or something?" I ask, breaking her moment.

"He didn't look."

"Go take a shower, sweetie," I say, going to her, hugging her. She holds me and I pull her close, kissing her forehead. "I'm going to find your father."

"Make sure you come back," she says.

"I will."

"Both of you," she says.

"For sure."

I'm tip-toeing down the stairs getting ready to head outside and find Stanton when the door to the outside world opens. My feet stop, my breath refuses to come. Then I see him. My Stanton. Relief pours out of me, but I'm terrible at showing it. I just don't have the energy.

"Do you need help?"

He looks physically exhausted, weariness dragging at his features and something like anxiety crawling through his eyes. Anyone can see the toll it's taking on him. What Stanton just did —the old lady's death, and those two boys pushing him to murder—it's left a palpable stain on him, one he might not be able to shake.

"She's rolled up in the carpet, just outside. I can't do this today. I need to get a shower and some sleep. I need something to eat."

"Let's go inside. Macy's showering, so maybe you can wash your face and hands, get something to eat, then rest. There will be plenty of hot water for a shower when you wake up."

"When I wake up, I need to find something to bury her with. And someplace. She shouldn't just be left on the sidewalk like some half-baked mob hit."

My mind goes to the little girl, the woman, the sitting dead man. That familiar ache deep in my breast for the toll this war is taking on this city and its residents.

"I'll help you."

"This isn't on you," he says.

Taking his face into my hands, looking at him eye to eye, I say, "We are husband and wife, a family. We are in this together, which means we share the responsibilities as well as the burdens. This isn't on you or me or Macy. We didn't do this. We aren't these kinds of people, but we're going to have to be for a little while if we want to survive."

"What if this is the end of civilized life, Sin? What if these are the people we'll have to become to survive this? I don't think I can do it. I can't be this way."

"Survivors survive by any means necessary, Stanton. We're not bad people. You're not a bad person. It was her time to go."

"I barely even hesitated, Sin. With those kids."

"And it's a good thing you didn't, because the more I think about the looks in their eyes, the more I think you were right to act so quickly and decisively. And they weren't kids, they were thugs. Armed bullies who threatened us. *All of us.* I shouldn't have doubted you, or questioned you. You were right to do that."

"I'm just not sure I can live with it," he says and there's a heaviness in his eyes I've never seen before.

I lean forward and kiss his cheek, then: "Well you're going to have to."

The night is fairly uneventful, except for the downstairs neighbor's on and off crying. Macy showers, Stanton lays down and rests his body but not his eyes. There's too much going on inside his head for him to doze off. I don't blame him. After an hour, he gets up and takes a shower, using up all the hot water, not that it matters.

"Is he going to be alright?" Macy asks.

"Are any of us?"

"Where am I going to sleep?" Macy asks.

"The couch," I say.

"I don't want to be out here alone," she replies, confiding in me. "What if someone tries to get in here? What if one of those things bombs us and you're hit but I'm not? Or me? What would you do if the bomb hit me and not you and dad?"

"We'll pull the bed out here, honey."

She nods her head, like she's grateful. And she is. Truth be told, I was thinking the same thing anyway. Macy just beat me to the punch in saying it.

By the time Stanton comes out of the bathroom, he's looking measurably better. Without saying a word, he goes into the old lady's bedroom and starts taking the bedsheets and blankets off the bed.

"What are you doing?" I ask from the doorway.

"I don't want to be in here while she's out there. I was thinking she could sleep with us, but this is a full and this bedroom is too small for the three of us. I can take the couch and I'll drag the mattress out here and you two can have the bed. At least all of us can be together. If that's okay with you."

I'm now wondering if he's not so lost after all. Nodding in agreement, I say, "Yeah, it's okay with me. But Macy can take the couch. You need the bed and I need you next to me."

As bone tired as all of us were by the end of the day, the onset of night had us itching to go to bed, even before the sun had fully set.

"When the last bits of daylight finally burn off," Stanton says, "we need to keep the lights out. We don't want anyone knowing we're here."

"The way things are going, I'm surprised they still work."

"If this keeps up, that'll change," he says.

Before the sun dips below the horizon and takes the day with it, I grab a piece of mail off the counter and text my brother Rex the address. I tell him to come if he can, that I love him. There's not much juice left in the phone and the screen has all but shattered from the recent events. I'm not sure if Rex will even get the message, but I pray he does because if this onslaught persists, it's better to have the people you love around you. No one will ever protect you as fiercely as your family, and vice versa.

The sun finally slides behind the city and just as everyone's starting to drift off, my phone beeps. I get out of bed, hide the light from the window and try to read through all the splits and cracks on the screen. The breath I've been holding finally rushes out of me.

"Did you just get a text?" Macy asks. I didn't know she was still awake.

"It's your uncle Rex."

I can feel her smiling in the dark. "What did he say?" she asks, happy he's alive and in contact with us.

"He's coming here tomorrow morning."

What it really says is, O THANK GOD UR ALIVE! BEEN WORRIED SICK. TRYING 2 FIND WAY OUT OF SF. FILL U IN 2MORROW.

The next morning Stanton and I get up (to the distant sounds of bombing), get dressed and head outside to deal with the bodies. Specifically the old lady. When we go outside, though, we find that the dead guy sitting up against the garage door is gone. Only the rolled up old lady, the woman and the little girl remain.

We're both looking at the little girl. I'm thinking about waving off the flies, but that won't keep them away. They're buzzing around the woman and the old lady, too.

"I don't think I can take her," I admit.

"I'll do it," Stanton says.

"I wish you didn't have to."

"Someone has to or she's going to sit there and rot. Or get eaten by coyotes when they figure out they can have their choice of corpses now that people are being exterminated and civility is a formality of the past."

"Don't call her that. A corpse."

"Yeah, but...she's starting to stink," Stanton says. He's not wrong. Then: "Sorry, Sin. You're right. I shouldn't be so blunt. It's just...all this, what's happening to us, San Francisco, it's starting to feel like—"

"Where'd the guy go?" I ask.

Stanton turns and looks at the dried-blood smears leading up to a vacancy in front of a garage door that's also smeared with the same rust-colored stains.

"He didn't just get up and walk away," Stanton says. I level him with a frown. "Sorry. I'm just trying to not be so bothered right now."

"Well good luck with that."

We scout out a place to stow the bodies. We settle on a row of bushes on the grassy hillside under the shade of twin trees at the foot of *The Exorcist* stairs that are formally called Arbol Lane for some reason or another. It's not a lane, it's an escape route. A serial killer's shortcut. The perfect movie prop for demons and priests.

Using the better part of an hour, we dispose of the old lady and the two guys Stanton shot yesterday. Stanton drags the little girl and the old lady down, too. He stops three times to gag and once to puke. They really do smell awful.

"If we kill anyone else," Stanton says, "we're going to have to find another place to stash the bodies because these bushes are full."

"This whole hillside is going to reek inside of a day or two."

"Blowflies and maggots will find them, and eventually we'll have to burn them," he replies. "Or not. Who knows what's going to happen in the next few days? So far, though, it's not looking promising considering the blue skies are now brown with ash."

"Will you try not to sound so morose?"

"If we're lucky," Stanton says, not even listening, "the coyotes will drag one or more of them off and save us the trouble of a bonfire."

"If I never think about what you just said for the rest of my life," I tell him, "it'll *still* be too soon."

As we're climbing back up the stairs, we hear the rumble of an engine. Motorcycle, not car, truck or drone. By the time we get up top, I see the sport bike and its driver parked in the driveway of the house we confiscated last night.

The rider pulls off his helmet, stretches.

"Is that Rex?" Stanton asks, looking at me. I smile and he looks excited. "How come you didn't tell me?"

"You needed a good surprise after all the bad ones."

Rex and Stanton are tight, even though Rex is twenty-three

and ex-military and Stanton is thirty-five and a soft money man. Well he *was* soft. Not now.

Not anymore.

"Hey!" I shout as Rex is getting off his bike.

He sees me, smiles, and we run to each other, into a ferocious hug that lasts forever. I can't keep him to myself though. Macy is outside now and Stanton is waiting.

The thing about Rex is he's competent, full of exciting stories and usually the life of the party when there's a party to be had. It doesn't hurt that he's super good looking either.

"Whatcha guys doing?" he finally says, looking at me and Stanton.

"Gardening," Stanton replies, still not his usual self.

As I'm looking at my hubby, I'm realizing I like him with a bit of scruff on his face and his hair a mess. It's totally the opposite of what he usually looks like. And Rex? His dark hair is short on the side with a little length on top, he has the same scruff as Stanton (although he's a few days ahead in growth), and he looks like he's been working out. Plus, he's clearly packing. There's a sawed-off shotgun on the bike, a pistol holstered on his side and a military issue knife strapped to his boot.

"You have any trouble getting here?" I ask.

"Yeah. Plus I'm out of ammo."

Looking at the pistol on his hip, Macy says, "That thing take nine millimeter rounds?"

He looks at her and grins, like he can't believe it. "When did you get so grown up?" he asks, looking at her then at me. We haven't seen him for nearly a year now.

"About fifteen minutes ago. We've got a box of fifty rounds if you need some."

That's when we hear the shotgun blast and duck. It came from inside the formless three story home we're staying in.

"What the—?" Rex says.

Stanton and Rex head inside, pushing open the ugly, white,

shot-to-crap door. Rex knocks on the first floor door, UNIT A. There's no answer.

"Hello!" Stanton says. "You okay in there?" Looking at Rex he says, "She's been crying all night."

Rex shrugs his shoulders.

"We're going to come in if you don't let us know you're okay!" Stanton says.

Nothing.

Rearing back, he gives the door a hearty kick and it caves around the lock. One more kick and he's in. Stanton turns around right away, a look on his face. My brother strolls inside.

"Depressed much?" Rex says as he's looking at the body.

There's what used to be a girl sitting on the couch, her body flopped backwards against the back cushions. Half her head is missing, the other half is on the walls at a meaty, forty-five degree rake. Macy tried to come in, but Stanton told me to keep her out.

"Go upstairs," I say.

"I'm not a kid anymore, Mom."

I turn and level her with my eyes. "You don't need to see this. Now go upstairs and get your uncle some water."

Reluctantly she heads upstairs, one heavy, stomping foot at a time.

Inside, the girl is on the couch. Blood-soaked grey matter is drizzling down the wall, which I find disgusting, even as a nurse. On the floor, laid out before her, is the guy who was outside. The dead guy against the garage door.

"Looks like we found the reason for her departure," Stanton says.

"Mystery solved," I hear myself say.

"We've got ourselves a modern day tale of Romeo and Juliet," Rex says.

Stanton fires him a look.

Rex once told me he'd counted up all his kills in Afghanistan. He started to cry when he told me they numbered in the fifties, and every single one of them haunted him. The fact that he's funny and upbeat all the time while holding on to this type of guilt makes me worry about his state of mind. I think it's an act. The upbeat, life-of-the-party part. I suspect it's a way for him to conceal the true pain eating him from the inside out.

Lots of ex-military can't take it anymore so they eat a bullet and call it a life. I pray every night my little brother won't end up the same way.

Rex starts nosing around the home.

"Guys, I'm not sure if you know this," he says, "but these people were prepared."

He's rifling through cupboards, checking the fridge and the pantry. He steps out into the garage and comes back grinning.

"We've got storable food, weapons, ammo and supplies, along with water filters and a bunch of camping equipment."

"Why would they need all that?" Stanton asks. "This is the city. We don't have preppers here."

"Really?" he asks.

On the fridge is an *SurvivorsGear.com* sticker. In the pill pantry are bottles of *Survivor's Gear* products. Some brain clarity product, a male vitality bottle and a black bottle of deep earth iodine.

"That explains it," Rex says, pointing to the black bumper sticker on the fridge.

"Survivor's Gear?"

"Yeah. It's a prepper's program on the internet. The people who run it are either on point or total nut jobs, but either way, they're always talking about being healthy and prepared for things like the police state and martial law. Looks like they listened, and thank God because what they have, it's not going to go a long way between the four of us, but it'll certainly soften the blow. Not the pills, I mean. The other stuff."

"They were prepared for everything but the loss of each other," I say with a heavy heart. I don't know what I'd do without Macy or Stanton. Probably the same thing the dead girl did. My eyes clearing, I ask, "What should we do with it all?"

"Where are you staying?" Rex asks. I point upstairs and he says, "Let's get it all upstairs then. Sort through it, start making plans for riding this thing out."

"Are you staying with us?" I ask.

"Depends on the neighborhood," he says. "What's it like? I mean, aside from all this."

"Quiet. Well today anyway. The drones went through here yesterday."

"Cool. I'll find a place nearby," he says. "Somewhere a little more upbeat than this oversized coffin."

"Why don't you stay with us?" I ask.

"The nightmares," he says, as if that explains everything.

I hear Macy tromping downstairs with a piece of paper in hand. She stands in the doorway, not looking inside because she's still pouting about not being invited in. A few of us look at her, and that's when she decides to hold up a handwritten note and say, "I think we have a problem."

CHAPTER TWELVE

Back upstairs, in the old lady's place, Macy hands the note to Rex, who reads it again: I KNOW WHAT YOU DID TO THE OLD LADY.

"What *did* you do to the old lady?" Rex asks.

"She...she didn't make it," Stanton says.

"Meaning?"

"Meaning she pulled a rifle on Stanton," I say, "and when he took it from her, she stepped backwards, tripped on the carpet and struck her head on the coffee table."

"This carpet looks a whole lot like a hardwood floor," he quips. Yeah, we get it, there's no carpet on the floor. No area rug to blame for the owner's absence from this place and life in general.

"No kidding," Macy says, arms folded, being playful. She adores her uncle, so I'm pretty sure it's just posturing so we don't have to talk about it. We don't really like to talk about it.

"So this carpet, the one that's *not* here—"

"We rolled her up in it," I say. "Then we sort of...found a place to stash her."

Suddenly it dawns on him—my smart, resourceful little brother. He gives a knowing grin and looks at Stanton.

"Ah," he says, "the gardening."

"Yes, the gardening," Stanton echoes.

Looking at Macy, pointing to the note, Rex says, "You want me to solve this problem?"

"That would be nice," I say.

"No," Macy replies. "I can handle it. I just need to borrow Daddy's gun."

"No," all three of us say at the same time.

"Whatever," she says before heading out the front door. Seconds later she's up there banging on the upstairs door. UNIT C, if the pattern follows. Me and Stanton trade worried looks, then both hustle up the stairs to where she's on the third floor kicking the note-writer's front door.

"Open up you sissy!" she's saying. "It's your pen pal from downstairs!"

Stanton gets to her first, grabbing her by the arm.

"This isn't the way we do things!" he snaps. "Downstairs, now!" Then to me, he says, "Take her downstairs. I'll deal with this."

He moves to the side of the door so whomever is inside doesn't get the bright idea to shoot through it and catch him in the chest. Macy breaks free of me, tromps downstairs and heads back inside our confiscated home. I hang out a few steps down.

"I'm sorry about that," I hear Stanton say into the door. He waits to see if anyone is listening. "I don't know if you've been out there, but it's really bad. All this...nonsense, it's turning people into, well...versions of themselves they're not."

There is nothing but silence. Then a creak on the floor. We both hear it. Stanton lets out his breath, takes another, then lets it out slower.

"We didn't kill her," he says. "But by virtue of us coming in here to avoid the attacks going on outside, she is dead and that... I don't know how to make that right."

The creaking again, then the sounds of feet walking away.

Stanton looks at me. With troubled eyes, he raises his brow and slowly releases his breath in either shame or dismay.

"It's okay, hon."

For the later part of the afternoon, we take the food, water and supplies from the downstairs neighbor's home. Meanwhile, the bombing continues unimpeded. Although the drones aren't targeting our neighborhood, we remain on high alert. When we make it through the day without incident, I won't lie, I whisper a short prayer of gratitude, thanking Him, or whomever is watching over us. God knows we needed the reprieve.

Rex shoves off that night with a bunch of food and water stuffed into his pant's pockets and the jacket he took from the dead guy's closet downstairs. As he's leaving, Stanton pulls him aside and says, "Can I see you outside? For a second?"

"Sure," Rex says.

"What are you two going to talk about?" I ask, making a very light, very rationed meal.

"Boy stuff," Rex teases. "No-girls-allowed kind of stuff."

He winks at Macy and I pray nothing bad happens to him. Growing up, you don't always like or appreciate your siblings, but as long as your home isn't some kind of a dysfunctional nightmare (ours wasn't), then you realize later on in life that maybe you love them and want nothing bad to happen to them. I love Rex like that. I'm glad here's here. But dammit, I really wish he wasn't going.

"When you find your home," I tell him, "make sure it's really, really close. And stay safe."

"Copy that," he says as he and Stanton head outside.

"Love you!"

"Love you too, sis!"

The front door shuts and some crazy part of me almost suffers a panic attack. What if I never see him again? What if something happens? What if—

"Are you alright, Mom?"

Wiping my eyes, going back to my dinner duties, I wave a

dismissive hand and say, "Mind your own business. Go to your couch."

That's code for go to your room, except she has no room, only three cushions and a stolen blanket.

"I have to use the excretorium first, if you don't mind."

Looking up, not sure what language she's speaking, I say, "What? You need to use the *what?*"

"The excretorium. The emporium of excrement? Hello...*the bathroom*. Oh, hell," she says with a monumental eye roll before going back to the bathroom.

"Just flush twice!" I call out as the door is closing.

The next morning we wake to the sounds of bombing. I wake up freezing, even though we're in a bed with extra blankets and everything.

I get up, pull back the drapes and two of the windows are broken from the intermittent shaking of the foundation. A few small triangles of glass rattled out, leaving us exposed to the elements. The smell of smoke hangs heavy in the air, but I'm slowly getting used to it and the headaches it's creating.

There's a soft knock on the door. I look at Stanton. He looks at me from where he's at in bed. His three day shadow is a little thicker today, his hair a mess and a half. Before we can answer the door, a note slides underneath it and footsteps hurry upstairs.

I grab it, pick it up and read it. It says: IT'S NOT OKAY.

I'm not sure what kind of juvenile game this person is playing, but I'm not going to be guilt shamed because one old woman failed to survive the apocalypse. Crumpling it up, I throw it in the kitchen where it lands next to the garbage can. By now Stanton is up, pulling a shirt on over his head.

"Are you cold?" I ask.

"No," Stanton grumbles. He's rubbing his hair, yawning, looking around the place probably wondering how he's going to fill his day now that he's got a roof over his head and no job.

"Well I'm am," Macy says from under her gigantic blanket.

"Window's broken," I tell Stanton.

Stanton throws Macy our blanket which she snuggles into with a welcomed smile. Then there's another knock at the door, this time not so subtle.

"What now?" I ask.

"Rex."

I open the door to my brother. He smiles really big, but I know him well enough to know he's looking for Stanton. They see each other and trade conspiratorial nods. Stanton's putting on his shoes. So now he's just a guy in fancy shoes with ash-colored slacks and a semi-clean white button-up, except for where it was exposed under his suit and has since turned gray. He runs a little water through his hair, halfway styles it, then takes a breath and looks at me.

"You look like a GQ model, *Walking Dead* style."

"I feel the 'walking dead' part."

"Where are you going?"

"He's borrowing my motorcycle," Rex offers. "Going into town to see if your guys' house is still standing."

I look at my husband, fold my arms and set my jaw.

"Were you even going to ask me?"

"I have to know," he explains. Clearly he's uncomfortable having this conversation in front of both Macy and Rex, but it has to be had.

"You need to be careful," I say.

"I will."

"It's not safe out there," I tell him, a bit of pleading creeping into my voice. "Will you at least take his helmet?"

"It'll keep me from having the best possible hearing," he explains. "If I'm going down there, I'll need every advantage I can get."

"I'll take care of you guys today," Rex says, smiling like he's being extra helpful.

"You know Rex, your charm and the apocalypse go together

like a fine wine and diarrhea. And we're not kids. Macy and I don't need babysitting."

"I know you're worried," he says, taking a step forward. I raise my hand. Yeah...stop means stop. Thankfully he's got the good sense to halt his advance.

"This isn't about us not being able to handle ourselves," I argue. "I'm worried about my husband. About the drones and how they've been bombing and killing people for days now." Looking at Stanton, who's looking extra sheepish right now, but determined, I say, "You have no idea how bad it is."

"I made it out of there before," he reasons.

"It's different now. We're several days into the bombings and these drones, or whatever, they seem very focused on downtown. Which is where we live."

"I know where we live," he says like there's nothing I can do or say to change his mind.

Knowing his stance on this, I go to him, give him a hug and a long kiss, then tell him to come back home to me and his daughter.

"She has a name, you know," he says.

"Yeah, I know."

He kisses me again. When he leaves, I pretend I need to lay back down, that I didn't sleep well, but instead I lay down, curl into a ball and cry. Macy pretends not to hear me. Rex pretends not to hear me. I pretend I'm alone and none of this is happening and thankfully, I finally do get some sleep.

Maybe a bit too much.

CHAPTER THIRTEEN

All throughout the day, as I'm turning in and out of sleep, I'm hearing the *pop, pop, popping* of gunfire. I'm hearing these harsh back-and-forth reports along with the distant sounds of things exploding. Then the sounds are near. Not the bombs, the gunfire. My eyelids crack open and I try with all my might to hold them open. I glance up and Rex is in the window, the drapes mostly shut.

Macy sees me awake and says, "They've been at it for awhile now."

"Who?"

"The cops and the dirt bags." I sit up, rub my eyes. She says, "Rex doesn't think the police are going to make it."

Rex says, "Buddies of mine say the Sureños hit the Northern District Police Station on Fillmore and Turk."

"That's like—"

"Seven blocks from here," Rex says. "Yeah, close."

I'm getting off the mattress, feeling out of sorts but straightening my rumpled clothes and gathering my wits about me.

"Where are they now?"

"Right around the corner. At that church. The Serbian Orthodox something or other." I join him at the window. He points to a peach-colored building across the way and says, "It's on the other side of that."

"This is bad, Rex," I say, looking at him.

"I know," he tells me.

"Is there a way to warn Stanton so he doesn't ride into the thick of it?" He shakes his head, no. "So then what do we do?"

"Hope the cops win. The problem is they're looking severely outnumbered. For every one or two volleys coming in, about nine are going out."

"Which means?"

"The Sureños have the high ground and plenty of weapons. There are about seven of them on the top of the church shooting down on the cops. With emergency services spread out all over the city, police and otherwise, these felonious douchebags apparently got ballsy enough to blow open the PD with an RPG."

"Wow," I say. "Felonious douchebags?"

"What's an RPG?" Macy asks.

"Rocket propelled grenade. It's a shoulder-mounted rocket launcher."

"Ah," she says.

"So after they blew a hole in the police department and gutted the armory, it would seem the cops ran them down and now we have a shootout a hundred yards away."

"Great," I mutter.

Looking at me, he says, "I know, right?"

"How long have I been asleep?"

"About four hours."

Later that evening, as the shooting dies down, then stops completely, there's a finger tap on the front door. Rex pulls his gun, I grab the old lady's shotgun, and Macy appears with her tactical assault sock in hand.

"Yeah?" Rex says into the closed door.

A muffled voice on the other end. "It's me, Stanton."

Oh, thank God!

Rex opens the door to Stanton. He looks like nine kinds of hell. Moving inside, he shuts the door behind him. He's covered in soot, blood from an open cut on his right eyebrow has dried in a long line down his face, his elbow is road-rashy and his pants are torn at the knees. He's even missing a shoe, which has his dress sock looking worse for wear.

"What happened?" I ask.

"What *didn't* happen? Good Christ. It's worse than a war zone. It's...it's indescribable what's going on downtown. Drones are everywhere. You look up and it's like the whole sky is full of them!"

"I didn't hear you come up," Rex says.

"Your bike?"

"Yeah."

"I stashed it around the corner. Not sure if you know what was going on, but all that gunfire was the cops basically getting slayed by a bunch of thugs holed up in a church."

"We've been listening to it all day," Macy says.

"I'm so glad you're home," I tell him with a kiss. "Now go take a shower then let me look at those wounds." What I really want to ask him is if our home is still standing, and if so is it inhabitable.

"Have you got something?" he asks. "Because there is all kinds of crap packed into the cuts. Dirt, soot, fibers from my pants and shirt for sure."

"I had a chance to go through that backpack that belonged to the couple downstairs. The medical backpack. It's like a hospital you can wear."

"I just need ointment, antibiotics and some Band-Aids."

"I'll be the judge of that," I say, relieved that he's finally home.

When he comes back out, he needs his leg stitched, his head wound glued shut and ointment on his elbow. Naturally I'm ready for him. It's not a pretty sight, but Macy steps out of the room and Stanton just sits there and takes it, grimace and all.

At the dinner table, by candle light, we eat and talk. Rex has gone home, so it's just the three of us. Ever since he walked into the house, I've been dying to know about our condo. I'm not hopeful, but until he tells me otherwise, I'm trying to stay positive.

"It's gone. Our condo, the building, the entire block. Even the Fairmont is sitting in a pile of rubble where it once stood."

I'd like to tell you I handled the news with a bit of grace, but I'd be lying. I don't take it well and it's showing. Setting down my fork, I walk away from the table, unable to finish the minuscule amount of food I'd put on my plate. Standing in the bathroom with the door shut and locked, trying not to hyperventilate, my body decides that now's the time to let it all out.

The prickle of tears hits me and I feel myself making the ugly cry face. Gigantic, warm tears leak from my eyes and my heart opens up with a kind of grief I can't explain. This moment makes everything real.

There is no home to go to.

No more things.

Our entire life was in that condo. All our valuables, my clothes and jewelry, Macy's baby books, our computer which had our whole photographed life saved on it. Pictures from our wedding, our honeymoon, vacations, the for-no-reason-at-all photos (my favorites)...everything. We even had an extra hundred thousand in emergency money in a floor safe that's now probably pulverized, according to Stanton.

When I'm all done, when my body is exhausted from the upheaval of emotion, I return to the table where Macy and Stanton are still sitting.

"So it's all gone?" I ask, hiccupping, my eyes still damp, my body feeling as weak as it's ever felt.

He looks up at me with heavy eyes.

"I'm sorry, Sin."

The three of us finish eating in silence. Well, the two of them let me finish since they're already done. Stanton blows out the candle as soon as my plate is clear, but none of us leave the table. Where else would we go? Besides, I can tell he's got something to say.

He's just not ready yet.

"I need to talk to you guys," he finally says. Then, after a long contemplative pause: "I know this new world scares you. It scares me, too. Whatever's making those drones do what they're doing, it's clear they don't want the city or its inhabitants to survive."

"We don't know that," I say.

"I talked to a guy down there who says the Bay Bridge is impassable. He says the drones have taken out the center section of the Golden Gate Bridge. He says they don't want us leaving. I can't argue his logic. I know this is me humanizing them, which I can't do, but they clearly have an agenda and it's not looking good.

"So what I want to say, what I *have* to say, is that we can't be the people we were last week. We can't afford to think civilized thoughts anymore or we won't survive. The word is that this isn't an isolated incident—"

"You mean other cities are getting hit, too?" I ask.

He nods, solemn, slowly.

"This isn't an attack on the city," he continues. "I think it's an attack on humanity, and though this might be a bit presumptive, maybe even an assumption based on not enough facts, it's obvious that life isn't going to be the same for awhile."

"Machines can't make decisions for themselves," Macy argues.

"Actually they can," Stanton tells her, and I know this to be true. "I pray that's not what's happening here, but the more this persists, the more it's looking like an extinction level event is underway. It's the only scenario that makes sense."

"That's a bunch of crap," Macy says. "Do you know how insane you sound right now?"

"Have you seen the National Guard? The Air Force? Any military assistance at all?" he argues, a little heat entering his voice. "Has the television or the internet returned? If no one has a clue about what's going on then it means they have no idea who's behind these attacks either, and if there's no clear enemy and no clear solutions and no help from the government or local law enforcement, what does that tell you?"

"That we're on our own," Macy quietly concedes.

"Exactly," he says.

"So what are we supposed to do?" I ask.

"Dig in, weather the storm, be the kind of people we were never taught to be, the kind we never wanted to be, the kind of people God would not want us to be if He could speak to us now."

"You want us to become...*savages?*" I ask, horrified by what I'm hearing.

A long pause, then: "Yes."

No one says anything for a spell, then finally Stanton breaks the silence. "We need to get a good night's sleep, then we have to fortify this place in the morning, talk about maybe finding someplace more permanent. Someplace more suited to long term sustainability under war time conditions."

So that was our big evening talk. Our big "come to Jesus" meeting. Stanton basically scared the crap out of me and Macy. Now Macy's asleep and Stanton's asleep and here I am, worrying away my sanity.

How much more of this can I take? *I don't think I can do this.*

I shouldn't have taken a nap earlier. It's thrown off my sleep schedule, which is beyond aggravating right now. The world is finally as quiet as a tomb, but I'm just laying here, cold, with no reprieve from my thoughts—thoughts that are quickly turning to some sort of anxious desperation.

Around two or three a.m., I hear a noise.

I get up, slide the curtains back a sliver, then peek out the window. A group of guys are walking down the middle of the street, not bothering anyone, but not in bed dreaming of sheep either. They've got backpacks and guns. They're dressed in warm clothes with beanies on their heads. Are they leaving town? Should we be leaving town, too?

Is there even a way out?

I go back to bed because it's freezing and my body is finally letting go. The heater struggles to a start and I'm thinking, thank God for the little things. It coughs out a few minutes later.

In the morning, I wake up to Stanton and Rex talking to Macy about the guns we have. She's standing in the kitchen in a shooter's stance with the Sig Sauer stretched out in front of her.

"You don't want to pull the trigger," Rex is saying. "You want to let out your breath, then squeeze."

"What's the difference between squeezing and pulling?" she asks, one eye shut, one eye looking down the barrel.

"Pulling raises the barrel, squeezing tracks better."

So for the next half hour she dry-fires the pistol, practicing on squeezing rather than pulling. And then it's me. After that it's a rationed lunch and more gun training. Then it's taking the weapon apart and putting it back together again.

When the afternoon is over and I'm feeling beyond tired again, Macy says, "So now that I know how to shoot a gun—"

"You haven't ever actually shot it," Rex says.

"Yes, I know. But now that you've taught me how to do it, do I have to give up my sock?"

"Keep your sock as backup, honey," I say, not sure if she's being smart-alecky or dead serious.

"She can get rid of the sock anytime she wants, Cincinnati."

"But it smells so good," Macy jokes, and then we're all laughing. Well, we're all laughing until the note slides under the door.

"I've had enough of this crap, Stanton," I say, the mood suddenly shot.

"I got this," Macy says, telling everyone to sit tight.

"Like last time?" Stanton says.

Macy snatches up the note, doesn't even bother to read it before stomping upstairs. Stanton grabs the Sig, goes and stands just outside the door, listening. When he comes inside, he says, "I think it's just some kid up there."

A half hour later, Macy comes back down with a boy her age, maybe a year or two older. "Guys, this is Gunner. He's waiting for his parents to come home."

Gunner is a tall lanky kid with shaggy black hair in need of a haircut. He looks painfully shy, and maybe a bit embarrassed.

"If they're not home by now," Rex says, "chances are pretty good they aren't coming home."

"Rex!" I say.

He shrugs his shoulders, makes a face.

"Sooner or later he'll see it, I'm just saving him time." Looking at the kid, Rex says, "C'mon man, you have to know what's going on out there."

He stands there, looking sheepish. Is it bad that I'm thinking, of all of us, he'll be the first to go?

"Speak up Gunner," Stanton says.

"I haven't been out of the house, but I've been sick, so..."

"So you know there's a war going on outside, right?" Rex says. "Man versus the machines and man is losing? That kind of thing?"

He looks down, his face losing color by the minute.

"Do you have food upstairs?" I ask. He looks up, nods. "Well if you run out, you come down and see us, okay? Same goes for water or medical supplies."

"Why would I need medical supplies?" he asks, his voice too small for the times.

"In case you catch a stray," Rex says.

"A stray?"

"Bullet. All that gunfire yesterday was the cops shooting at the idiots in the church. I'm talking about gang bangers, not parishioners, in case you're wondering."

"Oh," he says, then he turns and wanders out the front door.

"No more notes!" I call after him.

He stops, says nothing, then heads back upstairs. Stanton, Rex and I trade looks. Macy shuts the door then turns to us and says, "Talk about a dead man walking."

Rex looks at Stanton, then back at Macy with new eyes and says, "You know Stanton, I think little Macy here's going to be okay."

Let's hope so.

CHAPTER FOURTEEN

It feels like years have passed. Decades. In reality, it's only been a couple of weeks since the attack. With only one thing to do (survive), the days seem much longer, the nights measurably shorter. Surviving with no amnesty from drone flybys and the affects of the bombing, this war is taking its toll. Macy seems to be adapting the best, and Rex is solid, but me? I'm struggling.

But not as bad as Stanton.

Lately my husband has become increasingly agitated. I think it's from seeing the material summation of his life sitting in ruins. If we are our jobs, our houses, our cars...all our pretty little things, and they're all gone, then who are we really?

At some point in time, we're all going to have to figure this out.

To make matters worse, the water stopped working a few days ago. Talk about a devastating blow. What's next, the electricity? My mind starts thinking about spoiled food, lights, heat. So now we've rationing out the food a little better because, well...the attacks are ongoing and we're not sure they'll ever stop. If they don't, this city is bound to fall, and at that point you can pretty much say goodbye to the Bay Area for the next hundred years.

What has surprised us most is that it's not over by now. Maybe it will never be over. We can't stop it. And there's no fast food solution. No "call this person and get it handled" type of possibility of getting this matter done and over with. The drones seem to have an endless supply of ammunition and all we can do is hunker down and hope they don't bomb the neighborhood anytime soon.

It's inevitable though.

As for that easy solution to the drones? People have taken up arms against them. In the battle of guns versus bombs, however, Rex says bombs almost always win. He would know. He's done two tours in Afghanistan.

Some of the people we've talked to, those we've met (to their reluctance) on the block, they keep talking about things like emergency services, FEMA, the National Guard. After the shootout at the church, we found a slew of dead cops stripped of their uniforms, their guns and in some cases their radios and cars.

Now these scumbags have guns, badges and uniforms, so we don't trust that the cops are really the cops. We've been warning people about that, but mostly people are trying not to die of dehydration, starve to death or lose the roof over their head, the one that could be shelled at any minute.

The thing is, when you're on your own and the future looks dim, downright forlorn, most of these people aren't thinking about things like hope and long term survivability. That's why we don't talk to many people. We need to stay positive.

So that's my goal—not to lose myself, or get lost in all of this. I don't expect it to be easy, even though it's a noble, foolhardy cause, but this is my focus. So I try to set aside my fears and I try to stay upbeat, and most of all, I do my absolute best to have faith in the future, the odds be damned.

The way we've been planning for our future is by building our water stores and rationing our food. We're collecting dry goods where we're able to, and we're storing water for later. It's not safe here, though. We know that. What we need to do is find a way out of this city. Find someplace safe. Someplace rural.

So yeah, we've got lofty goals, but whatever. We're optimists in training.

Today Rex, Macy and Gunner are out scavenging for food and munitions. Stanton and I are on water duty.

In your standard residential hot water heater, on average, you can always find between fifty to eighty gallons of water. We know this because Rex knows this.

A few days ago, in an abandoned home two doors down, we checked their water heater and found it nearly full. No surprise there. It's exactly what Rex said we could expect. Using a couple of orange Home Depot buckets, we humped as much of the water back to our house as we could and started the purification process. In other words, we started boiling it. Pot by pot.

Once the purified water cools enough, we transfer it into our ever growing collection of sealed glass containers. The ones Rex, Macy and Gunner have been collecting. We've come up with a pretty impressive array of them by now. In fact, they're all over the home.

It's in this moment that I decide to mention the elephant in the room: Macy's constant pleas to carry a gun of her own.

Rex and Stanton are all for it. But me?

Not so much.

"Just because you think she can shoot doesn't mean she's ready for the soul swallowing burden of taking a life," I say. "You and Rex can't turn her into either of you."

This stings Stanton because it reminds him of the two boys, the old lady. He's still having a hard time with that, especially at night when there's nothing to do but ponder the things you've done, and everything you've lost.

"I'll tell you what I told her," Stanton says "which is exactly what Rex told me. And I hope you're internalizing this because this is how it has to be for all of us. If someone's in your face and you don't feel right about them, if something feels off, you have to shoot them. Don't even think about it. Just do it. Follow this rule, and we have a chance."

"You forget I spent my career saving lives, not ending them," I say, breathless and beyond uncomfortable with the idea of what I feel is unjustified homicide.

"Those days are gone, Sin."

"All I'm saying is she'll never be you or Rex," I explain. "She won't be able to do it, or handle herself if things get hairy."

Barely meeting my eyes, he just nods in complete silence as if to say, *Yeah? We'll see about that.*

"I just think you two are pushing her into this with a false sense of confidence."

I probably should have kept my mouth shut, but honestly, I've been too quiet about this for far too long now.

"Yeah?" he says, turning to face me. "How so?"

In the kitchen, four pots of water are now at a rolling boil, there are the consistent concussion bursts of buildings and houses being flattened, and there is the sound of automatic weapons being fired. Outside, birds don't chirp, dogs don't bark, and there are no planes or trucks or laughter to remind us of better times. Stanton is just looking at me, ready for an answer.

He's fully in the conversation now.

"All I'm saying is you can't lead her toward something she's not mature enough to handle. I don't want her killing anyone, Stanton. Not even if it's necessary. I know this doesn't make sense—"

The old stove flickers, then shuts off, then starts back up again. Both of us pause for a second, and then Stanton goes back to what he was saying.

"She's stronger than you think," he says, his eyes becoming a touch intense. "And more resilient than we give her credit for. I mean, her friend Trevor died in front of her and she hasn't gone to pieces over it."

"You don't hear her crying at night. I do. And when she's

making jokes during the day or being snarky or whatever, she's just like Rex. You haven't had a man that tough and that experienced in combat curl up in your lap and sob for all the lives he's taken."

"What's your point?"

"Hiding your emotions isn't the same as not having them. Things like regret and remorse sit like lead in your heart, infecting you, filling your head with nightmares, your eyes with tears and your soul with a terrible, impossible sadness. Is that what you want for our child?"

"You know I don't want that."

"I can't protect Rex or you, but I can protect *her.* That's why I don't want her having a gun. It's why I don't want her killing anyone."

"We can't tuck her away from this world, Sin. We can't wait until it's safe to bring her out of hiding. She has to learn it, the hard truths, the dangers, even if this world only lasts another week, month or year."

Turning away, feeling the sting of tears in the backs of my eyes, I say, "The water's done."

He shuts off the stove.

"I thought I was stronger than I am and look at what happened to me," I say. "Look at this blubbering mess I'm turning into. I never cried at work, or on the job. I mean, maybe once or twice, when there were children involved, or when mothers or fathers were taken from their family, but never like this."

"We're all handling the stress differently," he says, as if that helps at all. "Besides, you're different than me and Macy. You're strong, but you overthink the ramifications of what you *might* do, of what *might* happen. Have you ever thought of the consequences of not acting swiftly and decisively? Have you thought about what could happen if Macy was on her own and someone with bad intentions cornered her? Tried to hurt her, or take advantage of her?"

"You think I don't think about that? That's all I think about! I can't stop, Stanton!"

"Then you understand why I want her to know how to protect herself."

"You can protect us," I tell him, not completely believing this, but saying it anyway because I need to in order to clarify my position.

"That's where you're wrong," he says after a long pause. "Eventually, if we're in the wrong place at the wrong time, if we're overwhelmed..."

He can't finish, but I know where he's going.

"Is that why you're doing this? Is that why you're letting Rex train her? Because you're afraid you won't be able to do something if it really comes down to it? Because if we stick together, Rex included, she'll have plenty of protection."

He looks away, then back at me, then away again. Something in the air changes, grows a few degrees warmer, a little more suffocating. His eyes mist over. I know what he's thinking, what he's been thinking since the beginning. He's thinking about rape, about Macy's virtue. For the first time in a long time, I see the real him. The *scared* him. The *insecure* him.

"No matter how prepared or capable we are, or how willing we are to savagely slog through the mires of this sick new existence," he says with haunted eyes and resignation in his voice, "if someone wants to, they can hurt us. Badly. Kill us, even. Or worse..."

In that moment I'm pinned down by the hard edge of his greatest fears. I see them laid bare behind those rich brown eyes and it frightens me to know he feels this way. To know we feel the same. It's this fear that's been eating at me more and more each day. Apparently it's been eating at him, too—among other things.

"So this is the last time I'll talk about this with you or anyone. We are on untenable ground, Cincinnati, and we can't afford these tender moments. We can't afford to give fear, concern or even civilized reason an inch of ground lest we get caught off guard and killed. My only focus is on the survival of this family and if you keep taking me to these weak moments because you can't crawl out of them on your own, you're going to cut a hole in the only line of defense between this insane world and us."

I see his point. Still, I won't relent, not just yet. I'm not sure how to do this, and maybe Stanton is right: we have to protect our daughter. But we have to protect her not just from those who would look to take advantage of her, but from the things this new world might require of her. I can't have her shooting anyone.

In my most delicate voice, I say, "How are you going to feel when you look into her eyes after she's murdered someone and she realizes the gravity of her actions?"

He doesn't answer. The sickness of guilt permeates him. The loss of everything but his family and maybe a fraction of his pride is a weight he's now carrying openly.

The truth is, I'm terrified of what that day with Macy will bring. Will I sigh with relief? Will my heart fracture or will I swell with pride for her? Will I sob for the loss of her innocence, or will the circumstances be so harrowing that I'll feel nothing but joy that she's alive? All I want is for her to live, to survive, to lead a moral, happy life. That's why I can't let her grow up too fast. And certainly not behind a gun.

The day comes and goes with no more talk of killing or regret, and now it's nearly midnight. The bombing has stopped, the night is full and the sly creeping of a bitter cold has invaded our home, as it does every night about this time.

Curling into my blankets, relying on Stanton for body heat, I feel him. He's breathing slowly. He's awake. His body is nudged gently against mine, the heat of his skin a reminder that this war has failed to separate us as husband and wife, to break us apart as a family. It's the little things like this that fortify you, sustain you. But will this always be the case? Will this always be enough for me? For him? For any of us?

"I love you, Cincinnati," he tells me.

He always says this at night. Most times I believe he really means it; other times I'm convinced he's speaking out of habit while his mind is preoccupied by more urgent problems in need of solving. Tonight, I can tell (the way married couples often can) that dark things are tying knots in his mind. Darker things than normal. Eventually he rolls over on his back, laces his fingers in mine, kisses my neck and tells me to go to sleep.

This dog-tired mattress of ours sags in the middle and smells musty; these creaky springs have seen better days—just like my back, my neck and my hips. An hour passes. Stanton's breathing remains constant.

"What's wrong, honey?" I ask, knowing he's still awake.

"Can't sleep."

He takes his time telling me what's on his mind. Really takes his time collecting his thoughts. Twice I almost drift off waiting, but I don't. He's got something to say and if I'm asleep he'll wake me anyway. This is a man who talked a lot in his former career, in his once amazing job that is no longer. This is a man who needs to be heard.

"We're doing our best to survive," he finally says, keeping his voice whisper quiet. I wait for the rest, but the rest isn't coming just yet. His silence forces my mind to drift on passing tides. The truth is, I don't like having these conversations with Macy in the room. It's inevitable, though. We all share this corner of the living room for safety and body heat, and as I've told Stanton twice now, having her near keeps me from worrying so much.

Tonight, however, Macy is fast asleep. And judging by where this conversation might be headed, it's probably a good thing.

After an eternity of silence, I feel his head turning toward me in the darkness, his eyes surely lasered in on the shadow of my face. He brushes a strand of hair off my cheek, tucks it lovingly behind my ear.

"We're all dead, Cincinnati—you, me, Macy...all of us. It's just a matter of time. I know that now."

"Rex is planning an escape for us," I tell him.

"That's a pipe dream."

"It's not. He has friends in the city. Friends with resources."

"So he says."

The defeat in his voice is a wrecking ball destroying my resolve to press on, to live. When he says things like this, he has no idea the damage he's causing. How fear pumps mercilessly into my heart, and my indefatigable soul shrivels along the edges.

"I'm not sure how long we can do this," he admits.

"I know," is all I can say.

It's hard as hell to get any words past this lump in my throat. And I can't tell him the affect the turn in his mood is having on me. I just don't have the energy.

The words I ache to say lean on the edge of my tongue, trying to come out if only for that extra surge of...*what?*—anger, weariness, resignation? Every defeated bone in me is dying to call him a hypocrite, a selfish jerk, a quitter. I so badly want to say thoughts like these will get us killed. All three of us. But I don't. I won't. Had I said nothing about Macy having a gun earlier, he wouldn't be thinking about this. Maybe the way he's weakening me right now is the way I weakened him hours earlier. I shouldn't have said anything.

"I'm tired, Sin," he says.

"I know," I reply, still holding my tongue. "Me, too. Just go to sleep."

"It's not that kind of tired I'm referring to."

I know this, too.

Stanton was once a proud man, a market slayer in the business world and so confident about life that a woman like me needed no help falling hard for him. Over time he amassed a nice fortune for us, and a substantial ego for himself. I didn't mind as long as he didn't end up in some other woman's bed. What I did was play my part in the life we created for ourselves. Truthfully, I was thrilled to do so. We were the San Francisco success story every young couple ever dreamt of becoming. God, I miss those days.

I miss that life.

Thinking of how things are now, the three of us squatting in this parceled out hovel on the edge of a war zone, my stomach makes an epic turn.

As much as I don't recognize this life, I'm starting to recognize even less of the man beside me. It takes a little more of me than usual to remember the finer details of him. I try though. If anything to remind myself that when this is over—if it ever *is* over—we're going to find our way back to each other. And possibly back to ourselves.

My ears tune in to the sounds of Macy sleeping. She's balled up on the couch, her body turned away from us. Her breathing is deep, consistent. A few minutes later, Stanton begins snoring softly. Now that he's leveled me with his anxieties, with his defeat, now that I see the error of my ways, I'm left with the weight of his thoughts, the weight of this impossible burden, and the crushing weight of yet another sleepless night.

CHAPTER FIFTEEN

Once upon a time, our day used to begin with an alarm clock. Now we wake to the symphony of a rapidly declining civilization. The distant thunderclap of a city being bombed into oblivion is the new five a.m. rooster.

"I'd just about kill for waffles and bacon right now," Macy says over the noise.

She's curled up on the couch next to us, rubbing sleep from her eyes, a little dust from the ceiling sprinkled in her hair and on her shoulders like an advanced case of dandruff.

We all have it living here. The drywall dust. It's something we stopped talking about, and mostly because this is a symptom of aging homes perched on compromised foundations. When subterranean tremors rock these old buildings, sometimes a wall falls, or a ceiling collapses on you. Most times it's just a little dust raining down on you at first light.

"Am I the only one freezing here?" I ask.

"No," Stanton says, yawning. "You're just the only one talking about it."

When no one responds to Macy's plea for waffles, she says, "They sound close today. Don't they sound close today?"

I meet my daughter's gaze. I'm looking at her, trying to remember what she used to look like. A couple of weeks ago she was a slightly chubby, well-fed girl. She's dropped some weight now (too much), but she says it looks good on her so I'm not freaking out yet.

"Waffles sound amazing," I tell her, smiling even though inside I can't seem to shake this constant anxiousness. How you feel when you're right about to sneeze, but just can't get it out— that's how I feel about my anxiousness. It's like I'm on the verge of a panic attack *every single second of the day.*

"I know, right?" she says, getting out of bed. "Waffles with strawberries and whipped cream, and bacon."

Watching her, I'm overwhelmed with love. My beautiful girl. She's such a pretty child, and this scares me. Although beauty is good for the soul, the more restless parts of me know good looks don't always mix well with a lawless society. Stretching, pushing out a yawn or three, I work to fill my mind with more constructive thoughts.

Stanton's now at the window, turning his ear to the noise outside. He's listening to the concussion bursts following each explosion, trying to figure out if the attacks are moving closer or farther from us. Macy heads into the bathroom, closes the door.

Looking at him now, un-showered, unshaven, his black hair longish and messy, my mind wanders back to that first time he looked at me from across the restaurant. There was so much promise in that look. An unwritten future between us. Since that day, he's always made me feel cared for, spoiled even. Now the light has died in his eyes, like that impossible burden he's carrying has become too large for a man his size. Turning away from him, snuggling up in the blankets to ward off the early morning chill, I can't help thinking we haven't made love in three months. We always reconnected that way.

Whenever I bring this up, though, it's like it pains him to talk about things like love, a brighter future, the rest of our lives together. It's as if the very mention of personal indulgences is me ripping an old scab off a deep wound knowing how badly it's going to bleed.

Since we don't running have water, we pretty much pee down the bathtub drain, rinse it with a little water in a jar, and hope it goes somewhere, not just into the bottom of whatever pipes are down there.

A minute later, Macy comes out of the bathroom saying, "So about breakfast..."

"We'll eat in a bit, doll," I tell her. "Dad just needs to make sure it's safe, and I want to wait for Rex and Gunner before we even contemplate food."

"Might be an indoors kind of day," Stanton announces. "They're close. Plus drone traffic is a bit heavier than normal."

"Any pee-dee?" I ask.

"No," he answers. "Not that I can see."

That's what we call the new police: the pee-dee. The group of men and women formerly known as the San Francisco Police Department, or the SFPD...they're gone. These new cops, they aren't real cops at all. They're bullies with badges.

When the attacks first began, presumably the police leapt into action. Time and violence would have thinned their numbers though, and after that it wouldn't take long for everything to tunnel south fast. Odds are, half the force took off their uniforms for the last time. They had families to think of, homes to defend. Those brave officers who chose to remain in uniform and behind the badge hunkered down for the fight of their lives. These were the last real cops.

The now dead cops.

After what went down at the church, Rex said the biggest threat to law enforcement was probably the gangs. These days, on the block, that's all anyone can talk about. The Mission District threat. According to Rex's buddies, four hardcore affiliations rule the roost: The MS-13, the Central Divis Playas (CDP), the Sureños and the Norteños.

The word on the street is that it was the Sureños who

crashed the Northern District Police Station with an RPG. With this much confirmed, you don't need boots on the ground to know the Sureños raided the station. We're talking guns and ammunition, spare uniforms, medical supplies. And you want to know why people don't trust the cops anymore?

There's a saying you'll almost never hear, but one that bears relevance in this day and age: you're only above the law if you *are* the law. These self-righteous thugs stopped being a gang and instead decided they needed new colors, badges, and a new way to rule the Mission District post-apocalypse style. So they became the law.

Needless to say, Rex said if we see them, we need to hide. He says not to be heroes. He says we should shoot them before they shoot us, but only if there are less than three in the group. Anything more than three...*run.*

Stanton still thinks there might be good cops in those uniforms, but I think he's way off base. Of course, I've been wrong before. And it'll happen again. Either way, Rex tells us we have half a second to read their faces. I personally don't think that's time enough to fully clarify their intent, but it would have to do.

To Macy, he says, "You need to be sure. So as you're aiming, in that fraction of a second before you pull the trigger, you need to *see* them. Really get a read of this human being you're about to kill."

"Tattoos first, right?" Macy asked.

"You're not killing anyone," I say to Macy. To Rex I add: "Don't encourage her, please."

He nods, then says, "Before you launch *your* lug nut into *their* lug nuts, size them up by their stance and posture, get a quick read of their eyes and intentions. These guys will be wearing their false authority like a pair of stolen Nikes. They're as arrogant as the day is long, they're heavily armed and they have a gang member's mindset. This means they operate in packs and they don't treat anyone with respect. A real cop is different and you need to be able to *feel* this difference before you pull that trigger. Or launch that sock, if you will."

Looking at me, he smiles, like he's following my rules. But he's not. I don't want Macy fighting anyone, or killing anyone, even if it's with a stinky sock and a metal plug.

So that's the lowdown on the pee-dee, but we've got other problems. Like we're going through our food stores too fast. We're not rationing enough. And there are only so many homes you can break into looking for food before you choose the wrong one and get shot.

"Where are we going to search for food and supplies that we haven't searched before?" I ask Stanton.

I don't want to be too negative here, but lately my patience is for crap. Maybe it's because looking for food has become danger-ous, or maybe it's because I'm not sleeping well. When I dream at night, all I see are the insides of other people's homes and how we're always getting caught, or killed. I can't tell you how many times I wake up in the middle of the night sweating, terri-fied, crying.

"I have a few ideas," Stanton mumbles as he's surveying the neighborhood below. "Couple places that might have some stuff. I'm thinking we take another run at Jordan Park, or even Laurel Heights. It's been long enough. How many people do you think have died since we went there last? Surely there's an empty home with *something* to eat."

I don't even know who he's asking this question to, so I say nothing. Macy looks at me and I shrug my shoulders.

The way Stanton's talking, he sounds like he's a million miles away. Like he's speaking what's in his head, but only because his mouth is subconsciously giving voice to a host of barely-arranged thoughts. Why do I even bother anymore? If Macy and I leave the room right now, will he even notice?

It turns out the trip to Laurel Heights pays off.

We find a few bags worth of canned foods and a countertop water filter. A good one. We're talking stainless steel with the word *Propur* on it and two replacement filters (still packaged). When I saw it, what I saw was us not having to boil water all day. What I saw was less work for the same result.

Dinner isn't spectacular, but we've got food in our bellies and water to wash it down. Not a whole lot has gone on in the neighborhood either, and though this should give us a moment's peace, it doesn't. This is usually when bad things happen.

We've come to rely on the nights being quiet. Tonight, however, something wakes me. I'm not sure what it is that jolts me from my sleep, but when my eyes open, Stanton is out of bed, knife in hand, tip-toeing toward the door.

Rubbing my eyes, I sneak a glance at Macy. She's still asleep, thankfully.

"Stanton?" I whisper.

"Shhh," he says, now at the front door.

That's when I hear the soft wiggling of the lock. My breath catches high in my throat. A cold horror washes through me, leaving my skin prickled with fear. Is someone trying to break into our home? I keep waiting for my eyes to adjust to the darkness, but dammit they're taking too long!

"Should I get Macy in the closet?" I whisper.

Stanton's hand shoots up. He wants me to be quiet. Or does he want me to hold? Either way I'm sure he's every bit as scared as me.

For whatever reason, I can't peel my eyes from the outline of the big blade in his hand. It's a kitchen knife the old lady had for cutting...well, everything. It's not exactly lethal on the serrated edge, but the point is sharp and that's all that matters.

Suddenly the wiggling stops. My eyes are finally adjusting to the darkness, enough for me to see my husband at the door, listening, poised to attack, to defend this place.

For a second, I find my breath again.

They must have gone when they realized the door was

locked. Stanton looks over at me, like the threat has passed, and that's when the knob flinches just enough for us to know we're still in danger. Whoever's out there, there're not just checking the door, they're picking the lock.

This old door knob is keyed on the outside with a turn button on the inside. It's now turning, presumably moving from the vertical position to full horizontal. If before we were worried there might be trouble, now we're sure of it.

Oh, God. I can't breathe again.

The door knob slowly turns and Stanton readies himself. Using all the stealth I can muster, I'm off the mattress like a wraith, whisper-quiet as I'm grabbing the old lady's shotgun we keep on the floor beside us. I raise the weapon, spin in time to see the silhouette of a man creeping through the front door.

He doesn't see Stanton. I'm nearly overwhelmed with a shot of dizziness, one that thankfully goes as quickly as it arrived.

The second the intruder is inside, Stanton drives the knife up into the man's throat. For all the times I've questioned my husband's ability to operate at one hundred percent in tough situations—and there have been a few over the years—he seems to have picked up a thing or two about survival of the fittest. So instead of just sticking the man and stepping back, Stanton palm strikes the butt of the hilt brutally quick, jamming it farther into the man's neck; he then savagely twists the knife back and forth with both hands to do maximum, lethal damage.

This is Rex's doing. Stanton was never such a savage.

There's a gurgling in the intruder's throat, a wet sort of choking. Stanton yanks out the blade and the intruder drops to the floor in a violent heap. Stanton kicks him over; he topples sideways, all but dead.

"Drop whatever weapon you have or I put one in your head," a man growls from a giant pool of darkness just beyond the front door's threshold. There is gravel and apprehension in that voice, a certainty that he is not kidding.

I step forward, rack the shotgun and say, "If he gets it, you get it."

"You won't shoot me," the would-be intruder halfheartedly challenges, this disembodied voice in the darkness beyond the door.

"Grab your friend, get him out of my house or I paint the hallway with your brains," I snarl, my tone having never been more serious. It's intestinal fortitude powered by explosive terror and an indomitable will to protect my family, to survive.

"We just need a place to stay," he says, changing his approach.

"How many are you?" I ask. I want to know if this is going to be a bigger problem. I want to know if I have to go from pretending to be unhinged to actually pulling the trigger.

"Mom?" Macy says from behind me. Thunder crashes through me now, and I feel everyone go perfectly still. Everyone but the man with gun.

The man I can't see but in shadow.

I want to tell her to shut up; Stanton wants to tell her the same. Neither of us say a word because that's the kind of distraction that gets you killed. The kind of distraction that gets everyone killed.

"Me and my brother and his two kids," the voice finally says. Then: "Well, just me and his kids now that you've killed my brother. Do you just have the one?"

"Where are the kids?" Stanton asks.

"Downstairs," he tells us.

"Perfect," I say, working like the devil to force any anxiety from my voice. "When I get done with you, I'll hunt both of them down and end them, too. Now get your brother the hell out of our house or I swear to God, I won't wait for you to shoot him before I shoot you."

Thankfully I hear the rustling in the darkness, see a shadow bend over and grab the dead body's leg. Slowly the interloper is dragged from our house.

"This isn't over," he mutters.

"See, when you say things like that," I reply, "it means next time I see you I shoot first, then don't ask questions later."

Stanton shuts the door and we both listen to the man being dragged down the stairwell, shoulders and head knocking each and every wooden step on the way down. We hear the front door open. It bangs shut a moment later. Stanton peeks out the open window, scanning the street below. I join him, look over his shoulder. The two kids the would-be intruder was talking about are nowhere to be found. It's just the guy and his dead... *whomever—friend, brother, cousin?*

"Liar," I mutter.

"Scumbag," Stanton grumbles.

The tremors I managed to hold at bay overtake my body, leaving me jittery and high, too juiced on adrenaline to calm down. At this point I'm all fits and starts and it's terribly uncomfortable.

On the street below, the idiot that lived drops the one who didn't on the sidewalk. He heads across the street and starts trying other doors. He's a skinny thing with a lanky walk and a head full of ratty hair. He's a hundred and fifty pounds at best, maybe less.

"I'll keep watch," Stanton says. "You get some sleep."

"Will someone please tell me what just happened?" Macy asks.

Stanton turns and says, "What have I taught you that makes you think you should ever open your mouth in a situation like that?" The torrid break in his voice is fear and frayed nerves. To Macy, I'm sure it sounds like anger.

"I—I just..."

"She was scared," I tell Stanton, making little fists of my hands to still the tremors.

"You can't afford to be that stupid," he snaps. "You could've gotten us killed."

"I didn't mean—"

"Stanton," I say, calmly.

It's a warning for him to back off. He knows why, and he knows he should, but he just killed a man and this has yet to sit right with him. It's always like this after he takes a life.

"When it's this dark and you speak," Stanton says, his tone barely tempered, "you not only alert these men who broke into our home that you're here, you announce that you're a girl."

We've been hearing too much about all the rapes lately. And about the murders that follow. These are quickly becoming ungovernable times, dreadful times.

"Okay," Macy says.

"We were all scared, Macy," I explain. "Dad more than all of us because if anything happened to you, he couldn't bear it. Neither of us could."

"Did you at least have your gun in hand?" he asks.

"Yes," she replies.

"Are you kidding me, Stanton?" I say. "We talked about this!"

"And I listened. But listening isn't the same as agreeing, and I don't agree with you, so she keeps the gun and that's that."

As much as I hate that Stanton went against my better wishes, part of me is glad she was armed. And it was this situation that made me realize that Stanton and Rex were right about her having a gun.

"Next time," I tell her, "when your gun is out, your mouth stays shut. Got it?"

"Got it."

With nothing left to say, and the threat over, Macy lays back down, pulls the blankets over her. I crawl into bed as well because the house is so cold I'm practically shivering. Stanton sits at the table with the knife, contemplative as usual. I wonder if he's gathering up all the madness he feels. I wonder if the onslaught of emotions is swirling in his head like a hurricane, tearing up the landscape of his mind, eating away his humanity one kill at a time. To me, that's what it looks like. What it *feels* like.

As I lay there in bed, alone, replaying the events in my mind, working my way through the fears that set my teeth on edge, I can't help but acknowledge the rise of my darker impulses. Lately they've been crawling out of their black corners, forcing upon me thoughts I don't want to have, making me think I can do things I would never have done in more civil times.

I don't want to tell Stanton this. It's because of my earlier stance against violence. These days, my faith in scavenging for food is waning. I've been toying with the idea of taking what we need from someone who already has it. Someone like us. Someone alive.

Resorting to violence and larceny may gain us a few more months of food (the more civilized side of me reasons), but will we be able to live with ourselves if we steal from people like us? If we kill them for their things? Perhaps. If this keeps my family alive. And this is the thought that scares me most. It makes me wonder what I'm truly capable of.

"You sounded like a badass, Mom," Macy finally says.

"I nearly peed myself," I admit.

"This is never going to end," Stanton tells us both, turning the knife in his hand. His voice sounds so strained, so rippled with tension, I'm starting to think maybe he's losing it. Maybe we're all losing it. Maybe we've all lost it and we just don't know it yet.

A long time passes. Macy should be asleep. "Macy?" I whisper into the darkness.

"Still awake."

"Just checking," I tell her. To Stanton I say, "At some point in time, they have to realize they're wasting their resources on us."

"We're already broken," he says. "They don't care." Then after a minute, he says, "Does it smell like mold in here? It smells like mold to me."

"It's fine."

"It's not fine," he laments. "Do you know what mold can do to a person's immune system?"

"There are worse things out there than mold, Stanton." After awhile, when the silence feels so opaque it's all but unbearable, I say, "Thank you for protecting us tonight."

"You did just as much as I did," he says, nearly emotionless.

"Well thank you anyway."

CHAPTER SIXTEEN

The crush of noise and destruction wakes us all. That's how it is. How it's been every day since this nightmare began. Stanton's head lifts off the kitchen table, and at the same time, I pull the pillow over my ears. The attacks are closer than normal.

Sitting up, I wonder, is today going to be the day?

"Can we please go find something good to eat?" Macy says. "I'm tired of oatmeal in a cup."

So I guess Macy's awake. She's rolling over, sitting up as well. Her eyes look red and swollen, like she hasn't slept. I know *exactly* how she feels.

"Did you sleep okay?" I ask.

"No."

She's shoving off the blanket, putting feet into shoes that aren't hers—shoes that fit, but don't match.

When I was young, I remember reading about the forced labor camps in Auschwitz. When the Jews and Jewish sympathizers were transported into the death camps, those who died or were gassed, they were stripped of their shoes which were tossed into huge piles. When a person needed new shoes, soldiers grabbed two from the giant pile and threw them at the prisoners. One might be a size nine man's boot while the other could be a size six woman's heel. Someone once said more people were exterminated for foot related infections than for any other reason. I think they might be misinformed, but I can't be sure. It was probably just small talk with a sprinkling of exaggeration.

The point is, in times like this, you take what you're given and do your best to make it work. That's all we're doing—trying our best to make this work.

Looking over by the front door, there's arterial blood spray on the wall and a smeared pond of dried blood all along the old hardwood floor leading into the hallway. My eyes flick over to Stanton, see the dried gore on his hands and shirt, see it shot along the side of his face. He looks like the victim, not so much like the predator who put the victim down.

"You should wash up, Stanton. Just in case."

"It's fine," he says, looking at the blood under his fingernails. The man used to buy the most expensive hand lotions and face creams; now he's got some dead guy's blood in his hair and all over his face and it doesn't even faze him. This is massive progress for a clean freak. Does it seem crazy to you that I'm proud of him right now? Well I am, in a funny sort of way.

"You look like a horror show," I say. "And that beard has to go."

"The beard is staying."

"If you can't do it for you," I say, "at least do it for us."

He spits in his hand, uses it and his shirt to wipe his face. It only makes matters worse, but at least he's trying. Or maybe he's pitching a fit.

I can't tell.

Whatever pride I feel in him stalls the second another bomb hits. That's how things are now. We're living a minute-by-minute existence with no guarantees of anything, and that sort of trumps everything. Even these pint sized moments of satisfaction have the shortest of shelf-lives.

I drag myself out of bed, my skin breaking into gooseflesh

immediately, it's *that* cold. No one wants to talk about how cold it is but me. Same as always. Twice I nearly lay a fire, but I stop each time because Stanton will just tell me no, that we need to conserve our resources for when we really need them. What he's really saying is if the drones or the pee-dee see smoke coming from our chimney, one or both of them will level this whole place in no time flat.

From a small pile of confiscated clothes, I drag a sweater over my head, find my way into a dirty pair of jeans. My shoes are comfortable, but they're only a few walking miles away from splitting at the seams. Avoiding the bathroom mirror (as usual), I ask Macy to French braid my hair, which she does, then I scrape the fronts of my teeth clean with a fingernail. Macy and I check our guns, then check each other. After that we both look at Stanton, pinning him down with serious eyes.

"I'm coming, I'm coming," he grouses.

Like Macy, he's so skinny the sight of him hurts me. He's changing shirts. I look away, unable to take in the sight of all those bones, how he doesn't have much fat left on his body. I busy myself with something. Anything. If we make it through the day, I'm going to tell him he needs to start eating his fair share of food.

After a luxurious breakfast of oatmeal and water, we head outside in a tight pack of three, our senses attuned to everything, our minds ready for anything. You never know when people are going to crack. When they'll snap on you, or others around you.

Down by the Best Buy (bombed to all hell), this old woman with a grocery cart used to scream at everyone she walked by. She really put herself into it. Then one day she let go of her cart and went after a little boy. The mother of the boy shot the woman with a pop gun and just left her there to die. Sometimes, when I think about her, I wonder if the screamer was the lucky one.

Outside, the guy Stanton killed the night before is dead on

the sidewalk. Across the street his buddy is dead, too. Slumped over in the gutter, his chest a dark bloom.

"Wrong neighborhood to pick a fight, buddy," I mutter.

"You know Rex did that," Stanton says, nodding to the dead guy across the street.

"Is he coming with us today?"

"Not if he's still asleep," I answer.

Macy won't stop looking at the body in front of her. I finally grab her hand and say, "C'mon, honey. It's not polite to stare."

"I don't think he'll mind."

Over these last weeks, we've learned to protect what's ours. You need to do that. To think like that. So—first things first— we don't let people get too close to us without us showing them our guns.

Some say we're anti-social. I won't disagree.

We're staying inside Anza Vista just north of the Panhandle in our three story residence teetering on the edge of ruin. I don't expect you to know about that area specifically, but right now, you can't squat on our block without having big boy nuts. There's not a lot of us left, and we don't really mingle at this point, but if you don't belong in this neighborhood, you learn real quick to get out or get dead.

The reason I'm saying this is that we've been forced to protect this place so someone doesn't do to us what we did to the old lady who lived here before us. Stanton killed two people last week. He didn't even hesitate. That's how it's becoming.

That's exactly how it has to be.

The second trip to Laurel Heights was as good an idea as the first trip. That's where we found tonight's dinner. A near frozen pot roast. We even manage to make it back to our place alive, so there's cause for an almost-celebration.

Near dark, when the drones have all gone back to wherever it is they've gone back to, we lay a small fire. The warmth is amazing. Like sunbathing in Southern California on a ninety degree day by a hotel pool filled with beautiful vacationers. Except this isn't Southern California, there is no sun and the only thing beautiful about this place is the sunsets after a full day of bombing.

Honestly, the colors the destruction of this city makes at sunset are out of this world.

Sitting in the flames is the roast we procured from the bottom of an ice chest after about six or seven hours of rummaging through places much nicer than ours on Commonwealth Avenue. We're not sure if it's any good, but if it isn't, we'll eat what we can and toss the rest.

"Bowls?" I ask. The last light of day is quickly going away.

On the streets below, a couple of our neighbors are mingling in between the distant sounds of small- to medium-range artillery fire and the occasional blast of something big blowing up a little farther out. Maybe these are pipe bombs from the locals. Maybe it's the last of the bombing runs by the drones.

Stanton fetches us three mismatched bowls and we wait for dinner to finish heating. After a few minutes, with a pair of rusted BBQ tongs, I pull the meat from the fire, shave off the cooked outsides, divide it between us. It tastes overly salted, but then again, so does everything else.

What really scares us though, what we don't ever talk about, is that there's no new food. Pretty soon we're going to have to start hunting live prey. Birds, rabbits, dogs. Who knows? When you're hungry, you'll eat just about anything. Maybe even each other. Look at Venezuela. They even ate the animals at the zoo.

So one minute we're carving up more meat in silence, the next minute a bomb drops a block or two over, making the whole building jump. Fresh cracks snake up the sides of the wall. Dust falls like snow from the ceiling.

"Should I put out the fire?" I ask, hesitant yet cautious.

"It'll smoke too much," Stanton replies.

Sitting in filthy clothes, exhaustion nagging at my bones, I grip my bowl and Macy's hand and I wait. My heart is kicking way too hard. Can a healthy woman in her early thirties survive a heart attack in conditions like these? Most days I'd say yes; other days I pray for a quick death.

"Hurry up," Stanton tells Macy. "Eat in case we have to go."

"What about Gunner?"

He stands up, takes the bowl of meat upstairs to Gunner, then returns and says, "I invited him down, but he just shook his head and thanked me."

"He still hasn't come to grips with the fact that his parents are probably dead," Macy says. "And you and Rex scare him."

"That's because he's got sissy blood running through his veins," Stanton says.

"Hey," I say, "that's not fair."

By then, Stanton's already working on another cut of meat. I finish with mine and Macy finishes with hers. We eat until we're full, then put the meat in the fridge for tomorrow.

"Do you think when they get tired of this nickel-and-dime stuff," I ask, "the bombs will get bigger, maybe even turn nuclear?"

"I still want to know why they don't attack us at night," Macy says.

We've all been wondering it, and we have no idea. It's not like the drones need time off. They're not exhausted. They don't need to sleep.

"I don't know," I admit. "Rex says they don't have enough bombs to run 24/7. Maybe they're rearming themselves."

"What if they start?" Macy asks. "What if they make enough bullets and bombs to go all night long?"

"Then it's going to be pretty hard to get any sleep around here," Stanton replies, and that's that.

We don't continue this line of discussion because it will only take us down darker, more depressing roads. That's the last thing we need.

The sun is gone from the sky completely, the temperature dropping with it. Not too far from here, clouds of smoke billow into the already dismal sky. Night settles over San Francisco. Silence follows. Even small arms fire comes to a stop.

Hours later we're not so on edge.

Just before bed, while Stanton is still awake, the tears come. I try to stop them, but it's too easy to let them go. It's Macy that brought me to tears. This sniffling, it's all because I can't stop thinking that my daughter is just fifteen, that she doesn't deserve any of this. She's yet to be kissed, to find a suitable mate, to fall in love. She's got such a strong spirit...*she deserves these things!* I close my eyes, turn away, contemplate safer circumstances.

"Are you okay, Mom?" she asks.

"No," I say, "but yes, too."

Tonight I needed Stanton to not be his usual brooding self. I needed his body against mine, to remind me I am not alone, that he still cares, that we have a chance not only at falling in love again if this thing ever ends, but living our life to its end as a family.

To his credit, he slides his hands around my waist, curls into my back and says, "It'll be okay, Sin. I don't know how, but it will."

CHAPTER SEVENTEEN

Outside, you can't even see the sky anymore because the clouds are *that* low and it's *that* polluted. The air is just wet dust and compressed smoke. Also, I'm pretty sure we're breathing in asbestos. This beats the alternative though. People are getting slayed out there. They're being systematically murdered just for being human and alive.

"Do you think we'll have to leave today?" Macy asks Stanton.

"I don't know," he says. "I'm starting to think it's not good to put down roots for this long."

For some reason—and this started out as a concern, which became a synopsis, which has since been confirmed (based on entirely too much evidence)—we are being exterminated as a species. We're not sure there are any other viable possibilities left to consider.

"If you squint real hard," Macy tells me, her eyes on a triangle of blown-out window, "it looks like snow falling."

"That's great, sweetie," I say, my mind elsewhere.

"See what I mean?" Macy asks, dragging me out of my thoughts once more. She's pointing at the raining ash and calling it snow.

Is she losing her mind, or is this a silly game?

I bite my tongue, allow her this fantasy (delusion). She reaches out of the broken window, palm up, catching a few more flakes. She pulls them in, frowning when she sees they aren't wet or dense like snow. She rubs the flakes into her palm. They flatten into a dry, powdery smear.

"Come away from the window," I tell her. "Drones have been rocketing through here all morning."

Macy stays put, shoves her open hand outside again.

Looking at her, at her unwashed hair, I feel like the worst mother ever. She pulls in more ash, rubs it in her palm, then wipes the mess on her shirt. Her button nose and bowtie lips remind me that not too long ago she was a normal, well adjusted teenager.

"You're bathing today, Macy. No more excuses."

"Maybe," she says, preoccupied.

"You've never been a dirty child, do you want to start now?"

"I said I would," she snaps.

Even though she's well into her teens, and being a bit of a turd right now, all I see is my little girl. She's still so fragile my heart aches at the sight of her, of what she's having to endure. Of whom she must become to survive this impossible existence.

God I wish this part of me would just stop worrying!

The toll it's taking is too much.

You can't protect her from this, I remind myself. *You can't protect her from the entire world.*

Still, I'll shelter her and feed her as best as I can, and try to keep her from getting killed, but that's about all I can do. Standing in the kitchen, I can't even look at her anymore. Elbows on the counter, I lower my head into my hands, battling tears of exhaustion of frustration, battling tears of dread.

I know what's coming. How this ends.

I wipe away the start of damp morning eyes and stiffen my resolve against a wildly beating heart. But I can't seem to soften the lump in my throat, or the constant buzz of paranoia in my head.

"What are you thinking?" Macy asks.

"Nothing," I answer too quickly. *Trying not to go crazy.* Then: "Everything."

What I'm thinking, what needles at my brain, is that if we survive long enough, chances are good that one day we'll no longer resemble the people we were meant to be. It's already happening. We're turning back the years of evolution.

We're...*regressing.*

Suddenly I feel so sick to my stomach I can't help but think that suiciding us all in the dead of night might be the wise alternative. It was happening all over the place.

The suicides.

This couple below us, they were halfway ready for the holocaust, rogue governments, mass coronal ejections from solar flares and EMP blasts that squelched civilized society, but they weren't ready to be apart. Would they have been ready for this? For a loss of morality? The loss of not just each other, but themselves?

Stanton used to be level headed, a moral beacon, fearless with his money and his job title, undefeated with his silver tongue. I used to be even keel in the worst of situations. The ER prepped me for a lot, but it didn't prepare me for this. For the killing. For Stanton's bumpy fall from grace.

We all do it now. We can't help it. We're all taking our own little measurements of society. Notching out all those hashes on the wall, like some story we'll later tell our grandkids. Here is where the bomb went off, here is where we lost our house, here is where the city fell, where we lost our way, where we started killing and stealing and—

Ugh...my world is nothing but dark clouds. This morning I'm struggling to find hope. Will any of this ever get any better? Can we ever bounce back from this as a civilization?

I don't think so.

That's why suicide is my safety measure.

Knowing I have the power to spare us the indignity of such a bleak future, if things get that bad and there truly is no hope for humanity, I remind myself it's just three bullets and game over. This thought gives me a small degree of peace, although not as much as before. I don't want to die. And I don't want to have to kill my family.

But I will.

If it comes to that.

Ash drifts in through the broken window, settles on the floor. Outside the sounds of carpet bombing start back up.

"Shut the drapes, Macy," I tell her, my voice taking a stern edge. "And get away from the window."

Half the street-facing windows broke from a concussion burst a few days ago. We boarded most of them up, but we need a way to see outside, so we've left two open. We have only the drapes to shelter us from the elements, from the soot in the air. Most days it's enough. We lean plywood up against them at night, and it helps some, but the insulation here is poor.

God, those drapes. They're ugly floral patterned curtains.

I remind myself they serve their general purpose. At least, for now. Rex and Stanton have been talking about moving lately, to a bigger house, one that can accommodate all of us. I think that's why they're trying to get me and Macy good with the guns. Just in case…

For a second, I almost forget my fear.

Then there's a knock at the door—a sharp, authoritative knock that has us all paralyzed where we stand. Stanton rushes into the room, finds us, his flashing eyes telling us a thousand stories about how bad this situation could be.

"Hide!" he hisses.

"San Francisco PD!" the voice on the other side of the door barks. "Open up!"

Oh God, no! The pee-dee.

Macy and I hurry to the hall closet; I grab the Sig Sauer on the way, pull back the slide to make sure it's loaded. It is. Inside, we move behind the old lady's coats, our backs against the wall.

"Not a word," I tell Macy.

It's just me and my daughter in the dark, sweating, our hearts clamoring, our breath high in our chests and coming fast. Too fast. I pull my daughter's young body toward me, too forceful, way too fearful.

"He can't let them in," Macy is saying, panicked.

I'm thinking the same thing. But Rex said Stanton is in charge and we all agreed. Agreement meant compliance so no one would make the wrong move and get everyone killed.

The rifle stock hits the door again. "Open up or we'll kick it down and come in anyway."

Why these thugs still try to pass themselves off as cops seems preposterous. Apparently they're doing it because people are still complying. So as long as things keep going their way, success will shape their actions and they'll continue doing the same thing until someone stops them.

Can we stop them? Is that what Stanton's planning?

Out in the living room, at the end of a short hall, we hear the front door open and booted feet tromping in. The mix of authoritative voices puts my nerves on edge. The one thing I can't stop wondering is why the hell Stanton is obliging them. Is he thinking he can do what they want and they'll just leave us alone and move on? With everything we have, the truth is, we don't stand a chance against them. If they broke that door down and saw everything we have, they'd look for more and find us, too.

There was no way around letting them in and Stanton knew this.

Unconsciously I squeeze Macy even tighter against me, feeling her skin and bony frame, listening to her every quiet breath. Is she breathing too loud? If she yelps at some point, if she can't stand the anxiety anymore, there's a pretty good chance she'll get us killed.

Pressing my face into her hair, suppressing a hard sob, I

inhale the scents of her and wonder if this will be our last time together.

Tears flood my eyes. At this point, I've stopped trying to contain them. I'm cracking, just like Stanton's cracking, just like Macy's maybe cracking inside, but in a different way altogether.

The ruckus going on in the living room is the only thing keeping me from going to pieces. If someone opens this door...*oh God, I don't even want to think about that!*

Taking a deep breath, I find my resolve and realize that at some point I'm going to have to start killing, too. I can't just leave all this on Stanton anymore. It's time to pull my weight.

"Mom?" Macy whispers.

"Shhhh."

Rex and Stanton claim to be committed to the task of getting us out of the city, but it's proven to be more difficult than any of us had imagined. Listening to what's happening in the living room, I'm starting to realize it was all a big pipe dream.

Speaking of Rex, I wish he were here now. He's the merciless one. The determined one. The one with the combat experience and a penchant for bloodshed.

"Can't breathe," Macy finally whispers.

I don't realize how tight I've been holding her until she fights for that extra deep breath. My grip on her loosens, but I keep her close. If we're going to die here, it's not going to happen without one hell of a fight.

Another round of bombing rattles the world from a few blocks away, the walls rumbling, the floor beneath our feet shifting. I press a palm against the wall to steady us. Macy shifts her footing for balance, quickly but quietly. Some powdered drywall from above drops into our hair and lands on our shoulders.

We pay it little mind. I'm more concerned about the floor collapsing.

Heavy voices inside our home bark orders. It's amazing how authoritative they sound, how...police-like. They're mimicking even the simplest of details. Working quickly toward the goal of forced compliance. I hear Stanton's manic, aggravated voice talking back to them and I wince.

I can't help thinking, *this isn't the time to lose it, baby.* I can't help thinking, *keep it together.*

"What business do you have with us while blocks away we're getting shelled?" he asks. "We're nobodies. This whole city is filled with nobodies." Stanton is pretending that not knowing they're former gang bangers will save him. That it will save us all.

Will it?

"Get on your knees," the voice says, now monotone, completely devoid of empathy or humanity, "hands behind your head, lower your face to the floor, slowly."

"You're going to have to put a bullet in me before I bend a knee to you," Stanton finally growls, steadfast before them.

My body pulls in on itself, my muscles squeezing hard against the bones. There's the shouting of orders, my husband's crumbling foothold on life, and then *that sound.*

Their guns.

Their modified shotguns make a horrendous mechanical sound when chambering a round. It's a hard industrial *clacking,* that metal-scraping-over-metal sound of something that will easily shell out round after round after round of blazing hot death.

The sound is power. The sound is lives being ended.

We didn't expect the first round to blow through the drywall in the living room and end up cutting through the upper corner of the closet, but it did. Macy and I jump, but neither of us make a sound. Breathless, terrified, I check Macy, make sure she isn't hit. She's okay. Scared witless by the shaking feel of her, but okay nevertheless.

There's a scuffle outside and I hear the one in charge saying, "See, that wasn't so hard," and I know Stanton is on his knees, complying.

Keep it together, I'm thinking. *Please, please, please, Stanton. For us. For your daughter!*

Macy's head is jammed against my heart, which is slamming around in my chest with the fear that *they're going to find us.* When they do, there's no telling what they'll do. Actually I have an idea, and perhaps this is why I'm so scared.

"Search the house," the one calling out the orders says.

Things get pulled apart, overturned; drawers are torn from cabinets, flung about, kicked to pieces. I can't even imagine what they hoped to gain by destroying our things. But if they keep at it, if they tear through this house the way they are, they will find us.

It's inevitable.

Slowly I move Macy around to my backside as I step to the front of the tiny closet. My arm comes up, the gun goes out as far as it can, and when the door is finally jerked open, I see a man's face that isn't my husband's or Rex's and I just do it.

I squeeze the trigger.

He staggers backwards and I shoot him again, the ferocious jolt of gunfire startling me, unnerving me, damn near deafening me. Only for the slightest second do I realize the guy I shot is in uniform and he has no obvious tattoos.

Oh, no! I think.

I hear scuffling and realize now that I've played my hand, real cop or not, it's time to come to the table and up the ante. It's time to not be the me I've always been, but the me I must be in this world to survive.

I move out into the hallway, ready to charge whomever is out there with guns blazing. What I come up to is Stanton on his knees with a gigantic black shotgun pointed at his head. The barrel is pushing down on his skull and the man in the police uniform is frowning.

Beside him is another cop who has a shotgun trained on me. Both these guys have that hard look. Like time-on-the-street hard. Like time-in-the-joint hard.

"You just killed Clive," he growls.

His piercing blue eyes and slicked-back black hair make him

look like the Devil. Already I'm thinking of killing him. But Stanton will die if I do, then I'll have to shoot the other guy, but by then he would've already got me and that'll leave him and Macy.

The word *rape* runs rampant in my mind. I don't squeeze the trigger just yet.

"Did you hear me?" he asks, perturbed.

"I didn't kill him," I say, swallowing hard, "the bullets did."

The front door is still open. Can I make it? Get across the street to Rex before Stanton is dead and they get to Macy? No way. Stanton can't help himself. He's looking at me and I can see the defeat in his eyes. He's not wanting to go, but he's realizing he's dead and he's coming to accept it.

"Just shoot him, Sin," he says.

In a fit of rage, the fake-cop spins his weapon around, cracks Stanton on the head with the stock and from there everything moves fast and slows at the same time. The bullet I fired his way blows through the guy's jaw, but I'm already rolling for cover (a shotgun is fired, the explosion in this small space deafening). The last fake cop racks another load just as I'm coming up with the gun pointed at his face.

"I have you," I say. "You're down two, I'm down one, but I have you."

"I'm not down two, *we're* down two. There were three of us here *in here*, but there are dozens of us *out there*."

"You mean your brothers in blue?"

"My brothers. Period."

My arms are trembling right now. This is taking too long. I don't want to look over at Stanton, but the guy cracked him with authority and he's not moving. Whatever bravado I started with is melting fast as I'm realizing there's no way out of this.

He shoots or I shoot; one of us dies.

That's when I see Macy. She's creeping out of the hall closet with her assault sock at her side. She's looking at me, but moving in stealth and I'm thinking, *please God, no.*

The fake-cop sees me looking at her and he looks and that's when she steps out, the sock swinging backwards like a soft-ball windup.

"You know why I'm having a hard time shooting you?" he finally says. "Because you're too pretty to waste. But now that I see her, I'm thinking it's time for you to go. Because the fun me and her can—"

Just as his eyes are coming back to mine, his entire head roosters red in a shower of gore that fans out over a small slice of the entire living room.

The body drops face(less)-first to the floor and standing in the open doorway is Rex with a smoking shotgun and Gunner beside him, trying to peek in. Rex is pushing his face away because...*damn,* the mess that's been made is...too gory for words.

"If you can believe it, I think we've got our ride out of the city. Thank God for Gunner, though," Rex says. "Kid's got a pair of legs on him." Meaning he can run. Meaning he ran and got Rex the second he found a way.

"I had it under control," I tell him, my body starting with the post trauma shakes.

"What about Stanton?" he asks. "Did he have it under control, too?"

Looking down at him, Stanton's slumped over, blood soaking his hair and the floor around him. Panic wells in me and I'm on my knees in no time checking for a pulse. It's strong, thank God.

"Unconscious," I announce.

Then turning to Macy, my relief short lived, I say, "What were you thinking?!"

She blanches.

"I was thinking I could help. I mean, that's what Rex and Daddy have been trying to teach us, right? To work together to protect each other?"

"You could have gotten killed!"

"But she didn't, sis," Rex says softly. "None of us did and

that's always been the point." To Gunner, he says, "You coming with us or staying here?"

"Coming with," he says in a meek voice.

"Good, get your stuff, we're getting out of here. And double-time it!"

"Guess he's done expecting his parents to come home," I say.

Rex gives me a proud-papa nod. "Yeah, we finally had the talk a few days back. He cried, got it all out, and now he's looking like he's turning a new leaf. Not being so much of a milquetoast."

Stanton starts to come around.

"Get me a cold compress and the kit," I tell Macy. She's on it. "Just sit still," I tell Stanton, cradling his sagging body. "You're going to need stitches."

"He'll need to hold for a few," Rex says. "I've got us a ride out of the city."

I look up at him. "For real?" I ask.

"Time to blow this pop-stand," he says, grinning.

"Let me just stitch Stanton up—"

"Cincinnati," Rex says, softly, "we don't have time. We need to leave now if we're going to get to the rendezvous point. That's why Gunner didn't have to run far. I was already on my way over to tell you this."

I can't leave, yet we can't stay. I know this.

Taking Stanton's head in my hands, looking eye to eye at him, I can't believe we're going to have to go with him looking like he's lost in outer space.

"Just give me ten or fifteen minutes," I say.

Rex takes a hold of my arm. Roughly, he hauls me to my feet, grabs my face and turns it so we're eye to eye.

"You're not hearing me, we have to move, *now!*"

I shove his hands off me.

"We're not going like this!" I shout, grief stricken, so juiced with hatred for what happened my organs feel pulped, like they're boiling over with acid.

I would have died for him. I guess I planned on it the second

I shot the fake cop, the second I shot the second one, the second I saw Macy come out and realized if I died, she'd at least have another parent.

This man sitting before me is my whole life.

"How can I just let him bleed like this, Rex?" I ask, my voice so small, so wounded. I wipe away the start of tears, but the flood is as persistent as the pain of seeing him hurt.

"I'm so sorry, Cincinnati," he says, his eyes wild and jumpy, but unmistakably afraid.

Shaking off Rex's loosened grip, I sink to all fours, take Stanton's face and kiss him right on the mouth. Tears drip down my cheeks. His glassy eyes find mine; his mouth starts to move.

"Who's blood?" he's trying to say.

"Not mine," I answer. "And not yours."

I knew I caught some of the blood when fake-cop number three lost his head, but not that much. Looking down, my shirt is flecked with red spatter.

Macy brings me the medical backpack. "Cold compress, now," I tell her. She knows exactly what I'm talking about.

"We have to go, Stanton. You need stitches and we shouldn't move you, but Rex says there's a way out. He says we've got a ride."

He looks over at Rex.

"This true?"

"Took them a minute to find a clear route out of the city, and another minute to get the right vehicle for the run, but these guys are resourceful and good under fire. So yeah, we've got a way out."

In the background, bombs start to drop. They sound nearby. Too close. By the time we've got everything we need to move, the smoke and ash from the fires is like a fresh winter's snow, except it's gray and dry and will probably end up in our lungs.

"Ready?" I ask Stanton. He nods. "Let me know if you get dizzy, or if you start to feel sick, okay?"

"I'll be fine, Sin. It's just a cut."

"It's more than that," Macy says. "It's like a huge vagina on your head."

I draw a deep breath through my nose, try not to laugh, but also contain myself from screaming at her.

Rex isn't so discreet. He bursts out laughing while Gunner says, "Looks like it's on its period though," and then we're all in stitches. Well, everyone but Stanton, who's just looking at Macy shaking his head like he can't believe she just said that.

"On that fine note..." Stanton says.

On the way out of the house (I don't even see this, but later I'll realize what happened and it'll be too late), Macy grabs a holstered pistol from the dead fake-cop and tucks it into the waist of her pants, saying nothing, her expression giving nothing away.

CHAPTER EIGHTEEN

Half the city away, we see the first of a churning halo of fire lift into the sky. Is this one nuclear? Holy crap, it looks enormous! When the clouds spread out rather than turn into a giant mushroom, I realize our time hasn't come just yet, and this makes me even more determined to protect Macy. Within the hour, based on the moisture in the air and the low, dark clouds, it'll be raining sludge.

We should have brought some coats.

"Where are we headed?" I finally ask, the words sounding meek on my lips. "Where's the rendezvous point?"

"Diversidero and Turk," Rex says. "We're running late, so I hope they didn't leave us behind."

"Would they do that?" Macy asks.

"They're ex-military. They plan to the half-minute, so yeah... throw off their schedule and the whole op can sour."

"They didn't teach you flexibility in the military?" Macy asks.

He looks at her dead serious and says, "No."

The rain starts. It gets nasty shortly after. People are wandering through the wet muck in a haze of delirium, exhaustion. I had no idea it would be this bad. I keep an eye on the sky, but the drones don't seem to fly much in this kind of weather.

Silver linings.

We keep to the sidewalks, using the buildings as shelter, but I'm scared. This is emotional torture, this is fear ripping at me with the same force as grief, or loneliness, or the sense of having abandoned the home we'd just made our own. I'm frightened, devastated, crackling with anger.

Survivors of this war scurry from one place to another, one guy bumping into us and not apologizing, another woman pushing a shopping car with a plastic cover on whatever junk she's got stashed in there, some guy sitting on a curb holding his head, which is bleeding worse than Stanton's was and not saying a word about it.

The downpour is some unspoken signal to humans that it's safe to move. Without the drones, everyone gets brave. Traffic amongst the abandoned cars picks up quickly, too quickly for a few of these poor souls staggering this way and that. They look like malnourished zombies, some fighting with strangers, some with eyes as large as saucers looking to be somewhere. Just not here.

Not stuck at Ground Zero.

Maybe there are a million Ground Zero's. Maybe there is no safe zone. This city from top to bottom is hostile territory. But maybe every city is like this. Maybe there are people just like us in places just like this thinking the key to their salvation is a ride out of town.

Maybe we're all desperate fools.

The five of us don't slow our pace. We weave through the mayhem, hoping the weather keeps until we can get to wherever it is Rex is taking us.

Looking at Stanton, seeing that he's keeping up, I say, "You doing okay?"

He nods. I think he's in pain. Or thinking he should be in pain. Head wounds bleed a lot, but they don't always hurt so much.

We get to Divisadero and the street is pure pandemonium.

One minute we're all sure the raining sludge will stall the drones, but then they're suddenly there, ready to turn this place into a blood bath.

Everything leaps into hyper-drive. Panic overtakes the crowd. People start sprinting, smacking into each other and not caring. The drones are whizzing overhead, which freaks out everyone even more. Even the people in cars, where they can get through, roar down the sidewalks, forcing everyone to dive out of the way, even hitting a few unfortunate souls and not stopping to look back.

Short black missiles hiss off the wings of the drones, cratering a building wall. The air pillows in deep then explodes outward, damn near kicking us off our feet with a punch of heat and pressure we haven't felt before. We're running now. Even Stanton.

Tremors rock the earth as structures fall and dust clouds out everywhere. The very cityscape around us is changing by the second as we fight for our lives.

A building behind us, a three story home on the corner of Ellis and Divisadero takes it hit on the ground floor and suddenly its main supports are buckling and it's leaning hard. The entire structure starts to go. My eyes turn to Macy as she stumbles, the street under her shifting, separating. I grab her hand, pray she doesn't twist an ankle. The building hits and a *whoosh!* of atomized debris washes over us in a boiling, dirty cloud.

More drones zip by. Bombs destroy everything in their line of fire. An entire city block is leveled, and then in an instant, we're all dust-blind and stuck in the middle of a choking, brown fog. Fortunately the rain is there to repress it, but the air is nasty, coating us with all kinds of muck and filth.

Overhead the sky breaks completely open and what was once a drizzle quickly becomes a downpour that's dropping slop everywhere. The pasty mess is in our hair, our clothes; it's sticking to the insides of our throats.

The downpour doesn't last long. It tapers to a light drizzle and eventually we find cover. Hunkering down together, coughing, we're pulling our bodies close but keeping our weapons ready. By now, my concern for Stanton and his open wound is overwhelming. He lost the compress. It's now getting dirty.

"Mom," Macy cries out, her voice quivering in terror.

I look at her and her face is covered in soot, her blonde hair coated with the wet grime in the air. Mine must be just as bad. Worse.

"Are you hurt?" I ask. She shakes her head, no. "Then be quiet and keep it together."

"Are we going to die?" she asks two seconds before a bomb hits the row of homes across the street, adjacent to us by a few colorful structures. We're suddenly showered with the nearly vaporized remnants of someone's entire material life. We turn our faces and bodies away from the blast of smoke and shrapnel, struggle to our feet, wobble and totter our way through the destruction-filled haze.

The ringing in my ears is sharp, high-pitched and painful enough to test my will. Blinking hard, pawing at my face, I look at Macy and she's seems okay. Stanton, too.

And Rex?

It's like nothing happened. He's vigilant, focused, almost like he's at home in all this. What about Gunner, though?

"Where's Gunner?" I shout.

"With me!" Rex calls back. "Keep moving!"

We can't see much out here, and my eyes are burning as a result of the rampant destruction. At this point all I care about is surviving and staying together. Things are moving quickly, though.

A bit too quickly.

Trucks and SUV's retrofitted for urban warfare push through the chaos of people and abandoned cars and rubble, one of them mowing down an older woman hobbling through the gutters wiping at her eyes. Crushed and splayed out half a dozen feet from me, her head is completely twisted around, her spine broken in half after being run over.

The truck didn't even stop. For a second, I can't peel my eyes from her. She's just laying there half on the curb, and no one cares. The smoke rolls over her, bathing her dead body in a cocoon of wet ash. The way things are going, no one will move her, bury her or burn her. She'll just be left there to rot.

"Cincinnati, let's go!" Rex screams, dragging me from my reverie. His voice sounds a million miles away.

Through the diminishing fog of destruction come four cops packing machine guns. They look like pee-dee.

They don't see us, but they're hassling people along the way, shoving them aside like they own the street. One of the urban assault vehicles drives past them and they light up the back window with gunfire like a pack of idiots. The SUV veers into a mound of rubble and abandoned cars, slams into the side of a Buick and jolts to a stop.

Three people in the shot-up SUV kick the doors open and flee the vehicle. Drones race overhead. The smaller ones. One unleashes hell upon the driver; the other drone catches the remaining two survivors. The pee-dee open fire on the drones. Everyone hides. Even the crazies and the walking dead. One drone manages to evade the fake cops.

I lift the Sig, set my sights on this one drone. Rex pushes the barrel down, fires me a horrified look.

"What if you miss?" his hissing mouth says. He's angry because he's sure I would. He's convinced my anger will get us killed if I'm not careful.

I like to think I wouldn't miss, but target practice with a pistol in ideal conditions isn't the same as trying to hit a moving target under the strain of combat. I guess I just wanted to use it against them because of everything they've done to us. I'm suddenly consumed with the need for vengeance. Someone should have to pay!

The chaos becomes a brief silence that's quickly broken by

some intoxicated woman with huge jowls and a short mop of curly hair. She staggers out in the middle of the street, her face dirty as hell, her eyes turned up to the sky. She's shouting at the drone in Russian, cursing it, her mind obviously gone soft.

The drone circles around fast, fires a half dozen rounds, and the woman's head disappears, her body falling like a toppled tree. It hovers for a moment longer, looking on the now empty street. Then it's gone. Wow.

Suicide by drone.

Minutes later a huge, fortified SUV barely manages to avoid running over the decapitated woman before skidding to a stop. There's a guy hanging out the front passenger window with an automatic rifle spraying the pee-dee. The four clowns who shot up the SUV and took out two of the drones are slayed by a hail of this guy's bullets.

The felonious foursome is suddenly the dead foursome and that right there is a wonderful feeling. A hardened looking man who has clearly seen too much combat jumps out of the big truck, collects the pee-dee's weapons. When he looks up, he sees us and smiles.

"Rex, thank God man!" he shouts. "We were just headed your way. Grab what you can and let's go!"

My hearing, along with my balance, is coming back now. One look at Macy and I can tell it's the same for her.

"This is our ride," my brother says, half grinning, his face blackened by soot except for his eyes and flashing white teeth.

Our "ride" is a lifted black Chevy Suburban with large black wheels and a fortified brush guard. That makes this SUV solid, but it doesn't make it functional. Well, not until you consider the cow catcher. Attached to the frame just below the brush guard is a large triangular "shovel" like the ones they used to put on trains to push cows off the tracks when the animals ignored the warning whistles. Except this isn't a barred structure. This cow catcher is made of large steel plates, heavy welds and huge rivets.

The way it looks, you could probably push a building out of the way with this thing.

The five of us climb into the truck. Rex and Gunner are first in, taking the back seat. Macy, Stanton and I pile into the second row bench seat, pull the door shut and buckle up. The driver stomps on the gas, jerking us so hard my neck wrenches, and then we're off.

Macy turns to Rex and says, "Where are we going?"

"Away from here."

There's now an emptiness in her eyes I've never seen before. I wonder if she's looking in my eyes and seeing the same thing. How all of this is doing irreparable damage to our minds and our souls.

Wiping wet hair out of her face, cleaning some of the paste off her cheeks and chin, I feel pieces of my sanity being torn away.

"You doing okay, sweetheart?" I ask.

She just looks at me.

Her eyes are bone dry. Not a wet shimmer of emotion anywhere to be found. She must be so lost right now. Is she still in shock? I scrape more of the muck off her face, then pull her close to me and say, "Honey, I love you so much."

Something passes through her eyes, then: "I love you, too, Mom."

The emotions wreaking havoc on my already unstable sensibilities threaten to overwhelm me. I can't stop thinking about the cut on Stanton's head, how it's gashed open and packed with that crap from the air. I look at him now and his eyes look every bit as lifeless and Macy's, which is most likely the same way mine look. It's that empty stare, that perpetual unblinking.

"You okay?" I ask Stanton.

"Yeah."

He isn't. No one could be in times like these. Turning to Rex and Gunner, I see they are gripping for something so I turn around and see us coming up on traffic that's going to need shoving. The SUV slows for impact, then hits the outside car, pushing it out of the way.

The front seat passenger turns to me and says, "We mapped most of this out using a hijacked drone over the last few days, but it's gonna get a bit rough. As least until we push farther out. The going will get easier then."

"Thank you," I say. "For all of this."

He gives me a grin and a thumbs up, then he's eyes forward as the Suburban finishes shoving three or four compacts out of the road.

Smashing through the debris, rolling over the dead, grating past the carcasses of other cars and buildings, the passenger keeps a vigilant eye out for drones and presumably pee-dee (based on how quickly he shot the last four fake-cops).

Twice we hear the *plink, plink!* of rounds hitting the side of the truck. Everyone braces for more, but we're okay and the driver and passenger don't seem terribly worried. If they are, they're amazing at not showing it.

All along the horizon, the sky is the color of beaten concrete, the rain poisonous, but still holding at a steady drizzle. My heart sinks thinking of our situation. If the outside world is like this, we're going to die no matter what we do.

It's an eventuality.

The sound of something like a river rock hitting the metal side of the SUV startles me. The driver swerves and behind us a grenade goes off, blowing out the back glass and lifting the rear end a good foot off the ground. Grabbing a hold of what we can, we wait in horror for more grenades to hit.

Thankfully none do.

I turn and look at Rex and Gunner. Gunner's visibly shaken, but Rex is trying to calm him. It's not going so good since the back of his neck has pieces of glass embedded in it.

It takes what feels like forever to get to the edge of the city. The front passenger, who's proving to be as rowdy and as reckless as the driver, opens the window, hangs out with a restored

M5 and blasts a fake checkpoint. There are five guys who look official but most likely aren't. It wouldn't matter if they were.

The men in black clothing open fire on the vehicle but hit nothing that wasn't already reinforced for small arms fire.

"Hang on!" the driver yells.

By this time, bullets are smacking into the windshield's tempered glass. The driver has the gas pedal buried as we swerve to slam into three of the men, the impact of the truck hitting the bodies almost doing nothing to us inside.

We plow through the weak barriers; strands of barbed wire skid down the street in our wake. I turn and look behind us. The two men who were smart enough to dive out of the way as we crashed through their wooden barrier get to their feet and lay down a barrage of gunfire.

Rex tries to pull Gunner down, but it's too late. Gunner takes one through the neck and two through the back. This stills Rex for a second, but then he gives a hearty jolt sideways. Looking down at himself, he sees his own blood.

"Get your heads down!" the driver barks.

A dozen more rounds explode into the cabin. Macy and I duck. The front passenger takes one in the back of the skull. Rex is already slumped over, out of the line of fire. Now this guy in front of me is dead.

"AR 15's!" the driver shouts in warning, but then he steals a look around and sees the damage that's been done. "Son of a—" he roars, pounding the steering wheel.

Rex's arm is bleeding, his gaze distant, his face beyond stricken.

"Rex?"

Our eyes barely meet. He can't hold them. I see Gunner and my insides tear open at the sight of him. I can't look. I force my eyes back to Rex whose eyes are haunted and showing his pain. A lot of the color is draining from his face. He's back to staring straight ahead again, breathing fast and shallow.

"This your first time?" I ask.

He nods. Tough but distant. There's a dark, bleeding hole in his arm that's not so pretty. Macy averts her eyes, clearly afflicted. From my back pocket, I pull out a small knife, flick the blade open, cut a strip of fabric from the shirt sleeve of the dead guy up front.

Rex's face is growing whiter and more pasty by the minute. His already dirty forehead is now a shimmering mask of perspiration behind the rainy filth we've been forced to run through. I wipe his face clean. Scrub away the dark residue on his forehead.

"Lean forward," I tell him.

We're both bumping and jostling around in our seats, but I manage to get the strip wrapped around his brachial artery, not so tight that he loses feeling in his arm, but tight enough to staunch the blood flow. My only hope is that it clots and he doesn't suffer internal bleeding.

Fortunately the round ripped clean through and didn't shatter any bone, but it was going to hurt. Despite the brutal run through town, we push past old cars and lots of manageable debris while doing our best to avoid random gunfire. No one says anything about Gunner, or Rex, or the front seat passenger.

Then again, I can't speak because the pain of losing Gunner is that sharp. I'm proud he made it this far. Sad that he's gone.

"He's the lucky one," Stanton says, and it becomes clear he's thinking of the boy, too.

Looking at Rex, I feel a stab of pride. Not for getting shot, but for keeping it together on his first time. A lot of people go to pieces the second they see their own blood. And Stanton? He hasn't spoken a word of complaint.

"Can you still feel your fingers?" I ask Rex.

He nods.

"Keep light pressure on the wound," I shout over the drone of the engine, finding something inside me—a toughness I'm going to need now that he's been injured and is no longer in charge. He nods his head, the wind blowing a few strands of his hair around, his eyelids sort of low over his eyes.

The memories of our youth come flooding in, unbidden. It makes me wish we were back in those times. Back then, we were too happy to even consider the future we might now be forced to endure.

"Don't pass out," I say, taking his hand. Is he really about to pass out? "Stay with me, Rex."

Right now, all my training as a nurse means nothing. In the ER, things aren't always the epitome of control, but at least you weren't racing through a city ravaged by ten thousand enemies in an atmosphere rife with chaos, death and sloppy rain.

Rex nods slowly, his head lolling to the side as he passes out.

"Are you freaking kidding me?" I mumble.

I grab his shotgun, set it on the seat between me and Macy, my grief held at bay once more. Now that we're out of the main war zone, the going is a little easier, even though the Suburban is sustaining irreparable damage and is now making a harsh clicking sound in the engine. Rather than worry about our ride, I focus on Stanton (who says he's okay), and Rex (who's still unbelievably unconscious). I'm thinking of checking his field dressing, assessing whether or not he's going to need a full tourniquet when the driver screams, "Drones!"

He turns to the dead passenger, then his eyes flick up into the rear view mirror looking at Stanton, Rex and then Gunner. His eyes finally land on me, only to find I'm looking right at him. He passes me a plastic black box and says, "When I tell you, push the red button."

I sit up straight, keeping the driver's face in the rear view mirror in sight. It's a battle tested face for sure. Almost handsome. Certainly flush full of adrenaline.

"This is a detonator?" I ask. He acknowledges me with a quick glance and a nod, then his eyes are back on the road. "To what? A bomb? IED's? An exhaust-pipe flame thrower?"

"Just push it when I say," he orders. He's checking his side mirrors, slowing the truck, waiting for the right moment.

Looking backwards, I see a platoon of light attack drones

moving in from on high. My eyes go to Macy, who's looking at me. She's cradling the shotgun, which looks huge next to her. This image will be seared into my mind forever: Macy with this cannon.

Clearing my thoughts, pushing aside my grief, my fear, I tell myself this isn't the end, but I don't believe it. No one survives the drones. Up ahead, it looks like the Presidio and the ocean beyond that. It's a beautiful last sight.

"I love you so much," I turn and tell her.

"You keep saying that," she says, her eyes finally showing signs of life.

It's because I keep expecting this to be the last time I can tell her. If Gunner's death proved anything, it's that one second you can be sitting here, breathing, being alive and everything, and then the next second you could just be slumped over, full of holes. I don't want to make the mistake of taking Macy's life for granted. Or Stanton's or Rex's either.

"Is he really out cold?" Stanton says, looking at Rex.

"Yeah."

"What a bitch," he mumbles.

"Stop it," I tell him, even though I can't believe Rex spent half a decade in the middle of the war and couldn't handle being shot in the arm.

With the drones closing in on us, my brother and my husband injured and our lives in the hands of a stranger behind the wheel of a truck that may or may not be eviscerated when I push this red button, all I can do is pray.

Taking Macy's hand in mine, I can't get a sunny thought to enter my mind. I look at her, memorize every feature as if I haven't already done this a million times before.

This is my daughter, I tell myself. All that's left of me. This is the girl I will die protecting, if only dying was enough. Looking down at the red trigger, I fear what's ahead. What pressing it will mean.

"Now!" the driver screams.

Squeezing my eyes shut, bracing for...something...I press the button.

Our truck dies suddenly, all power gone. Eyes back open, I look behind us, out the broken window, in time to watch the drones fall from the sky. EMP. Electromagnetic pulse. Meaning I just killed anything and everything with electronics in it, including this truck.

A deep sigh escapes me. My relief is palpable.

"We need to go," the driver says, grabbing a few things before kicking the door open with a booted foot. With him, there's not a moment to spare. For a short second, I think: definitely ex-military.

Rex is coming back around, but that's only because I'm half hanging over the seat shaking him awake. Shoving his shotgun back into his hands, I shout his name directly into his face. His eyes flutter. Doing the only thing I know how to do, I slap his cheek with all my might.

"We have to go! Now, Rex!"

He wakes up, takes my extended hand then sits up and crawls out of the truck, wobbling a bit before staggering onto solid ground. He nearly falls but manages to stay on his feet.

"You're like a newborn calf," I tell him. He smiles, but it's weak. He has no idea where he is.

The four of us and the driver are on the move, not a single word between us. We clear the main road, hustle past some burned out houses, make our way into a field of damp, waist high grass.

Rex seems to be coming around. And Stanton looks like he might be okay, too, although I'm not sure where we're going. The rain drops to a light mist, still it's wet and nasty and it's making a bad situation worse.

The driver's on the move, cutting through the field faster than we can keep up. He breaks into a run. We follow his lead. He looks back, puts on a slight burst of speed, but not so fast that he loses us. He knows we're trying. He also knows Rex and Stanton are holding us back.

"Keep up with him," I tell Macy, not sure how much more we're going to have to keep this pace, if where we're headed is a destination or if we're running from everything coming after us.

Macy doesn't do as she's told, as usual.

She hangs back with me while I'm hanging back with Stanton and Rex, now certain they'll both get us all killed. Stanton being out of shape and injured, and Rex being off his game because he's been shot, is telling.

Up ahead, through a clearing in the only expansive patch of green in sight (although it's coated with a glob-like layer of wet ash, so it's not as much green as it is a muted sage color) is a large helicopter, an old-school Huey painted a flat, forest green. Already its rotors are turning, the noise of the engines rising to a roar.

When you can't escape the bombing raids, when the city seems to be suffering the mother of all apocalyptic events, when low level radiation may be the weather forecast and at any time you'll either be killed by drones or assassinated by gang bangers posing as cops, the only escape is to escape the city itself. This was Rex's plan for us and he's come through. Now, God willing, it appears we might survive this thing after all.

Something in me feels reinvigorated. Like this wasn't all for nothing.

I think of Stanton who said we were already dead, and I think of this world that's trying with all its might to end us, and then I think that we're finally leaving this war zone behind. It's a good feeling that doesn't last long. In the back of my mind, I can't help thinking we're also leaving our home, our jobs, the grand summation of our lives. Is this what going savage means? You can only care about the things you can reach out and touch?

"I'll hold our ride!" I shout before picking up speed. "Don't stop!"

Grabbing Macy's hand, knowing Rex will make it even if he's

not moving at a hundred percent, the two of us fight to catch up to the driver. After all, he's our ticket out of this place.

I let go of Macy's hand because I can't sprint at top speed like this. "Stay with me!" I shout over my shoulder.

My run becomes a full out sprint. If the three of them can't keep up, I can at least get there fast enough to stall the helicopter, giving us enough time to board.

I'm fifty yards behind the driver when he jumps into the Huey. He puts a headset on, leans forward and says something to the pilot. A smile creeps on my face for a fraction of a second. Right now my lungs are burning. I have a stitch in my side and my limbs are protesting, but I'm going.

We're going!

The ride out of this cesspool of death and destruction is going to be a new life for us. A fresh start. The driver then makes a circling sign to the pilot with his forefinger, the classic sign for, "Let's go," and my heart all but sinks. The big helicopter lifts out of the grass, sending sharp waves of dread coursing through me.

No, no, no, no, no!

My lungs are skewered with pain, but that doesn't stop me from screaming, pleading and cursing. I pull to a stop directly under the helicopter, under the damp, churning winds and it's still leaving.

Some kind of visceral moan for being left behind escapes me.

I drop my hands and just stare up at the belly of the thing, and that's when four drones appear from where we've just come. There are two large ones armed with missiles accompanied by two light artillery drones. From inside the Huey come the boisterous sounds of heavy caliber automatic weapons' fire. The two largest drones go down, but not before one of their missiles is loosed. Seconds later the Huey explodes, turning sideways in mid-air, then falling out of the sky and crashing onto someone's home in a fiery wreck.

The whirring of the remaining drones ignites my nerves. I keep my eyes fastened to the two of them now knowing why the driver wanted to leave so quickly. The EMP had too short of range to catch all the drones and we couldn't wait any longer to set it off before facing certain death.

And so we missed these ones.

Macy reaches me, but in the distance, Rex and Stanton slow to a walk. I'm screaming for Rex, telling him to look up. I'm pointing at the approaching drones.

Rex sees them, turns as best as he can and starts shooting despite his injury. With the shotgun, he hits the first one, wobbles it, then takes out the other, but not before going down hard in the field and disappearing in the tall grasses. A mortified whimper erupts from me.

"Rex!" I scream.

The wobbled drone is diving earthward though, heading toward Macy and me and now Stanton is running for us, screaming. Macy and I start backpedaling, then turn and run for our lives as the thing plows straight into the earth behind us. We're both diving out of the way the minute it slams into the earth and comes to a stop.

Getting up, with the Sig Sauer and the last of my strength, I put two rounds into the downed drone, then drop the gun and pray to God I don't go to pieces. But it's happening. I can feel it. If Rex is dead...*oh, Rex.*

"He has a plan for us," a voice inside me whispers.

"No He doesn't," I hear myself say, fresh tears standing in my eyes. "There's no plan at all, unless death is God's plan."

Stanton reaches me in a hug. I barely even feel it. I'm about to run to Rex when Macy does something neither me nor Stanton have ever heard her do: she breaks into a wild, cursing fit of anger that soon becomes a brutal crying jag. All I can do right now is hold her and tell her everything is going to be alright, even though it won't be.

"We'll catch another one," I say, composing myself for my daughter's sake. "One that won't blow up."

"No we won't," she says through a fit of hiccups and sobbing.

"I have to see about Rex," I hear myself saying. I'm moving out of Stanton's arms, saying, "He could still be alive."

"Are you kidding me?!" she cries, looking at me with sopping wet eyes. "He's *not* alive! He's dead like everyone else!"

"Macy," Stanton says.

I try not to think of all that's happened—of my injured husband, of Gunner and my now dead brother—and I try not to think about how I'm going to survive this world under these conditions, but I have to. Maybe not now, not in this moment, but I have to look ahead and create a way where there isn't one.

Macy pushes off of me, her eyes still soaked, her chest shaking, the persistent sounds of her crying reminding me she may be fifteen, but she's still so immature.

Nearby, I hear the sounds of more drones.

"Run!" Stanton yells, pointing to a grove of trees nearby.

Beyond him, around the clearing, also taking cover from the drones are five men with guns. What the hell? I can only think one thing: the helicopter going down and the shooting must have attracted attention. But then I think something else. I wonder, are they here to help, or will they be a problem?

By the hard looks of them, I'm thinking they could be a problem.

CHAPTER NINETEEN

Wasting no time, Macy, Stanton and I run for cover, which is really just a canopy of trees weighed down with the gunky residue left behind by the toxic rain. I don't know if other drones will find us here, or if the men in the field will follow us. I hope not. We're not exactly safe anywhere. At least we're not out in the open though. Crouching down at the base of a tree, Stanton joining us, we wait in absolute silence. Seconds tick on.

Entire minutes pass.

"I think we might be okay," Stanton whispers. His head wound has opened up again and is bleeding, but I'm not as concerned about the blood as I am the possibility of infection.

He really needs that thing clean and stitched up.

It's in this brief moment of safety that I start to consider all the other dangers around us. If the drones don't kill us and the bombs don't kill us and the gangs don't kill us, chances are pretty good—when enough people get hungry enough and desperate enough—that our own kind will set upon us as a last resort.

This is what we've feared most: the moment society turns on each other. I'm surprised it's not worse than it's been, but the truth is, it's bound to get much worse before it gets better.

If other cities are enduring this the way we're enduring this, then that begs the question: will we live long enough to see "better?"

If civilization has truly fallen, can we come back from this?

For all of our insecurity about our future, for all our fears, Rex has given us combat wisdom and Stanton has blessed us with his business acumen. Rex got us this far, but now that he's gone, we need to rely on Stanton and Stanton seems to have the right idea about how to handle things.

Crouched down, waiting for a clearing, and a plan, I can't stop thinking of something Stanton said a few days back. He said the apocalypse is proving to be a lot like the business world: if you're not the hunter, then you're bound to become the prey.

As I sit here feeling like prey, I realize our survival depends on me becoming the hunter. For whatever reason, maybe because Rex is gone and Stanton is injured, I find myself stepping up to the task. Standing up, I tell Macy and Stanton it's time to go. I'm not exactly sure where we're heading, only that doing something—even if it's the wrong thing—is better than hiding here and doing nothing. We can always self-correct.

"Slow down!" Macy says as we trudge through the trees and meadow grass toward a clearing, and a neighborhood. "Wait!"

Stanton and I turn around and level her with raised eyebrows.

"Where are we going?" she asks, like she can't grasp the reality of this situation.

"We're going to circle around and see about Rex, and after that, I don't know. There's a hundred houses to choose from. Maybe a thousand. Basically we're going to find some place where we can clean your father's head wound before it gets infected and we have to amputate."

Wait, holy crap. Did I just say that? Wow. Talk about terrible gallows humor! Even for me. Stanton and Macy just stare at me. I don't blame them.

Then after *that* awkward pause, I make a proclamation. "We're leaving this godforsaken city one way or another. I'm not sure how we're going to do it, but mark my words, it's happening."

Macy looks up at me, then beyond me, and what my daughter can't say in that moment is that we might not be going anywhere. Seeing her eyes shocked wide open, seeing myriad emotions cross her face in lightening quick progression, I turn and follow her gaze.

Not fifty feet away, tromping out of the same grove of trees are five creeps with guns and hard eyes all the sick signs of trouble. To both my relief and my horror, they have Rex. He's on foot and alive! But he's being held at gunpoint and not looking terribly happy about it.

"This gringo piece of *mierda* here says he doesn't know you people," the guy holding him hostage says, "but the worried look on that cute little blonde's face clearly says he does."

This scumbag, this bald thug with a tattooed face and piercings and a criminal's sense of fashion (white sneakers, grey slacks, white tank top), he clanks the barrel of the shotgun on Rex's head one, two, three times.

"Yeah, I knew by the look," he says to me, head turned sideways, chin jutted forward and pointing a finger at me, "I saw it in your eyes, you guys are lovers."

Rex shakes his head and says, "That's my sister, bro."

"So that's your niece then," he says, the tone full of meaning.

Everyone starts to snicker, not boisterous, but like they're in something that will be good for them, but not us. You don't have to be a genius to know what any of these fools is thinking.

"Looks like it's play time *ese,*" he says, his body saying yes to all the many things he's thinking.

My blood is officially boiling.

I can't stop the rage building inside me and I know right now I need to keep a cool head. But the way his predatory eyes are giving Macy the once over, it turns my stomach and ignites something in me, a violent protectiveness I can't explain. To my sheer horror, looking back at all the times we've been confronted by men, their eyes always go to me, to Macy. Is this a symptom of the future? Will my daughter's good looks always make us targets?

Refusing to show fear, I lock eyes with him, and only then do I become afraid. There is nothing in those eyes. No sense of right or wrong, not an ounce of benevolence or humanity, only an emptiness born of greed and the need to hold everything around him in a stranglehold of his own making.

He sees me seeing him, thinking this, and he laughs. It's a sanctimonious chuckle that tells me all I need to know: he has no soul.

We're screwed.

Looking from Macy to me, and never really at Stanton, he says, "You two girls are going to clean up nicely. I can tell. You're going to be the two prettiest princesses we've ever had. We're going to pass you around over and over and over again (pointing to each of his boys as he says this) until your insides fall out from all the fun we've had with you. And then you won't be pretty princesses anymore. You'll just be a couple of mutts we pulled off street."

Beside me I feel Stanton tense. I already know what he's going to do, which is why I flash him a look.

Two or three of this scumbag's pals snicker, grabbing my attention. They're all a bunch of soulless cretins, entertained only by the humiliation and tormenting of others.

In situations like these—unimaginable situations, downright terrifying situations—you can't even find the words to say, much less utter a single intelligible sentence. This is why Stanton shot those boys back on *The Exorcist* stairway. Now that the roles are reversed, the choice becomes easy. I would shoot every single one of these men in the face.

But five on four? Not so much.

Instead of pulling my gun and going all *Butch Cassidy and the Sundance Kid*, I find myself tumbling through a flurry of horrifying possibilities. I'm looking at the men promising to rape me and my daughter into oblivion and I'm thinking of all the viciousness I'm going to unleash, but then I realize it'll do no good because his friends are like him in that they like the fight, that they *want* the fight, and so whatever I have, I know it's not enough.

It won't ever be enough.

"Look at Daddy over there," the scumbag teases, "looking like he's wanting to come out of his skin. You wanna watch, pretty boy?"

"I think he wants to join," someone else says with laughter in his voice.

I grab Stanton's arm, knowing he's being baited, wordlessly begging him not to take it. I feel his muscles relax the slightest little bit.

The torrent of possibilities ripping through me quickly becomes just one acceptable truth: whatever's about to happen, it's going to be bad. And if by some miracle we survive to see the other side of this thing, we won't be the same people. We won't even know who we were before all this.

"My God," he says looking right at me, wonderment and humor in his expression. "You just rose up against me then fell into defeat right before my eyes. We haven't even had an ounce of fun yet and already you're beaten." Turning those ugly, hooded eyes on Macy—not even bothering to mask his intentions—he says, "Let's pray this little slice of heaven has more fight in her than her mother."

"Come here, sweetheart," he says, all eyes on Macy. Macy turns her scared eyes on me.

Frantic, a wicked frenzy building inside me, I turn to Stanton and he's got that murderous look tucked away behind almost blank eyes.

"Stay put," Stanton tells her.

I look at Rex and he's looking defeated, although I pray that's not the case and he's just playing possum.

"Don't look at her!" the guy holding Rex barks at Macy.

I look at Macy and her eyes are dancing with fear. Macy doesn't move, but inside I'm preparing for war. No way this prick is taking my daughter.

"I got an idea," he says, racking the shotgun and jamming it into Rex's face. "You get your little titties over here or I swear to God almighty, I'm going to pull the trigger and make a mess of your uncle's face."

"Mom?" she asks.

"Do I have to count to three?" he snaps, impatient, irritated that none of us are complying. No one says anything and you can see just how much this aggravates him. "Okay, fine. Let's do it the hard way."

Pause.

"One."

I look away from Macy to Rex. He's playing possum better than ever and this concerns me. Is this a ruse for him, or is he really afraid? *Oh God,* how hurt is he?

"Stanton?" I say.

His cheeks are trembling with rage and his eyes are obsidian stone. Is he getting ready for this? For the guy to just kill Rex before he makes a move?

"Two," the creep says.

That's when the cushy *boom!* in the sky draws our attention to the heavens. It's different from the concussion bursts we've been hearing closer into the city—the sounds of missiles destroying buildings.

Then, all the way up Presidio Avenue, the bulbs in the overhead street lamps explode, the shattering glass tinkling all across the asphalt.

In the distance, down the hill, transformers blow and fire runs down the phone lines in showers of sparks.

That's when the first arrow comes. The guy with the shotgun to Rex's face, the one with the dirty mouth and a head full of sexual depravity, his skull is suddenly skewered. The arrow goes in the temple and exits just above the hinge of the jaw. Meat and drizzle drip off the razor sharp tip.

What the hell?

He staggers backwards a step. A knee buckles and he topples over into the weeds, but not before Rex can snatch the shotgun out of his hand. A second arrow sinks into a throat of a second man and Rex is already firing on the third. The shotgun blast has us all jumping, but not before three new guns are drawn.

Of the five ruffians threatening us, three are down, leaving two. The quietest man is the one who surprises us most. He never said a word, never cut loose in laughter, never put his eyes on either me or Macy in a malicious way. But now he's got two guns out, lightening quick: one on Rex, another on Stanton. He quickly positions himself in between Rex and Stanton, using Rex to shield himself from the incoming arrows.

Another arrow rips through the air, but the gunman now knows where they're coming from so he inches to the right and arrow flies by. I go for my gun, but he says, "That gun comes out, this guy gets it in the face."

With the pistol, he motions me over toward Stanton.

My hand comes away from my weapon; I move toward my husband, but only slightly. I keep waiting for Stanton to do something, or Rex, but moving on this guy means someone dies, so I understand why they haven't moved, and how terrifying this is.

"Who's your little friend?" he asks, turning his body sideways to keep both Stanton and Rex in sight while shielding himself from the mystery archer.

No one answers.

I'm on the edge of his vision, but apparently I'm no longer a threat. Is there a way I can draw on him? Catch him off guard?

"Either of you heroes decide to move on me, I don't ask questions. I just shoot. Not to any of the adults though, I changed my mind. The first bullet gets the girl. Now everyone move in front me where I can see you."

With the shotgun aimed at this guy, Rex says, "Stay put. He shoots me he's done. You hear that? You have a bullet. I have pellets."

"I know the drill," he snarls. Another arrow zips by startling the gunman, but not enough to knock him off his game. Looking at his buddy—who also has a weapon on Rex, he says, "Get the others, tell them I have dessert, but come heavy."

The fifth guy takes off running.

Macy is moving now, one inch at a time out of the gunman's view. Inside, I'm freaking out because in her hand, behind her back, is a handgun. Something I never expected.

Where did she get that?

Just as another arrow rips through the air, Macy's got the gun out in front of her and I can't breathe. Looking over, Stanton can't breathe either. Time slows to a crawl. A smile curves Rex's mouth into a grin, and the guy's eyes slide sideways and find Macy.

She doesn't speak. She just shoots him twice in the torso.

By now the fifth man is at the edge of the street. He turns to see what's happened, but by then two arrows are headed his way. He sees them, drops and rolls out of the way, both missing their mark. Hustling to his feet, he sprints in a zig-zag pattern down the street.

Two more arrows head his way, but both miss.

"What the hell, Macy?" I scream, but she can't hear me over the thunder in her ears.

And the guy face-down on the ground? She's walking right up to him, a cold hatred in her eyes like I've never seen before. She aims down and fires, putting a bullet in the back of his head. Just like Stanton did with those two bullies on *The Exorcist* stairway.

I stifle a cry, but it's not enough.

The dam inside me breaks open and that's when I lose it. That's when I go to pieces because Macy's innocence is now gone. She's no longer a child. No longer my little girl.

Stanton's got me in his arms, and Rex is taking the gun from Macy, who just saved our lives. He's telling her she did good, giving her a hug. She has that faraway look, but Rex isn't letting her bathe in it. He's talking her through it, telling her she just saved us.

I glance up and a young woman with a bow and quiver of arrows is walking our way. She's tall (maybe five foot nine?) and thin but not frail. Her chestnut hair is pulled into a ponytail, a few strands hanging loose in her face. She slides the bow on her back and I can't help but be impressed. Or scared. There's nothing soft about this girl.

She's wearing black boots with black jeans and a black skin-tight tank top. Her body is lithe and competent, her look slightly athletic. The closer she gets, the more I can see her eyes. They're like cold stones: steadfast, unfeeling.

Yet she came to our rescue. My tears dry up as curiosity quickly replaces loss. All four of us watch her as she approaches.

"You guys okay?" she asks.

Her voice is a summer rain; it's kind but strong, tempered yet poised to say more. We're strangers though, and in the company of strangers you're never really your authentic self.

"Thanks to you," Macy says, still rattled. "That was amazing."

"Do you guys know what just happened?" she asks. "It's like all the street lights were shot out at once."

"I think it was a power surge," Stanton says. "But from the sky."

"Nuclear EMP," Rex concludes.

"EMP?" the archer asks.

"Electromagnetic pulse," Rex says. "Detonated at the right altitude, we're talking about a devastating weapon. The energy is powerful enough to knock out the power grid for hundreds of miles around."

"Isn't that what the Iraq guy told us might happen?" I ask. "The guy who gave us the extra ammo?"

"Waylon," Stanton says.

Rex reaches out his good arm, extends his hand. The archer looks down at it, wary, then takes it. "I'm Rex McNamara, this is my sister, Cincinnati, her husband Stanton and their daughter, my niece, Macy."

She looks around and says, "Indigo."

Looking at her, feeling an immense swell of appreciation, I'm too overwhelmed to just stand here. I go and take her in a hug, which she hesitantly returns.

"Thank you for saving my family," I tell her.

"I've been hunting these guys for days now." That's all she can say. This one is a great shot, but she's light on words.

Turning to my daughter, who is now standing next to Stanton, I say, "Macy, sweetheart, are you okay?"

"Yes, why?"

"Because you just killed that man," I say, unable to escape the fact that this dark day has finally come—the day I warned Stanton about, the day I've long since feared.

"No, Mom. I didn't kill him," she says. "I saved us." Then, looking at Indigo and Rex, she adds, "Well *she* did. And uncle Rex did."

"It was a group effort," Indigo says, unsmiling, and we all agree. "Did you have anything to do with that helicopter going down?"

"That was our ride," Stanton says, finally speaking up.

"Drones?" she asks.

"How'd you know," Rex replies, sarcastic.

The way my brother is looking at her, I can tell he's smitten. It never fails to surprise me how the world can come to a complete stop the second a guy sees a pretty girl. Then again, this girl isn't pretty in the girlish sense of the word. It's more like she's tomboyish, and capable. Two things a guy like my brother appreciates. *Obviously.*

"Why were you hunting them?" Macy asks. "Who are they?"

Indigo leans down to the one with the arrow in his head, pulls up his shirt and on his ribs is the tattoo of a large black snake that's accordioned in a series of S's. It's dark, scaly and menacing. Worst of all, the ink looks fresh.

"They call themselves The Ophidian Horde. They're a new gang from what I've gathered. Offshoots of the SoMo gangs and fresh out of the wrapper."

"SoMo?" Stanton asks.

"South of Market."

"Like the Mission District gangs?" Macy asks.

"Yeah, I guess. I think they formed out of...whatever it is that's happening, or happened, here. The last two I tried to talk to, they didn't make it." Looking at Rex, she asks, "Why did the EMP go off? Who would do that?"

"Most likely the military. No other way to stop the drones."

"You enlisted?" she asks.

"In between tours in Afghanistan. I was heading out in a few weeks, but I'm thinking that's all a moot point right about now."

Indigo grabs a hold of the arrow in the man's head, gives it a tug, testing it. It doesn't budge. She gives his head a little kick, then goes to the second guy. Bending over, she yanks the arrow out of his throat, sloughs off the blood and meat, sticks it in the quiver on her back.

He starts to squirm a bit; he's not dead. Not taking her eyes off him, she reaches a hand back and says, "Gun." Macy hands over her weapon; Indigo fires a round into his forehead then turns and hands the gun back.

"Thanks," she says.

"Uh...you're welcome?" Macy replies while the three of us just stand there slack jawed and speechless.

While collecting the other arrows that missed their targets, to no one in general, Indigo says, "So where are you staying?"

"Off of Turk," I say. "But we were ambushed by guys like these. We made it out alive, but lost one along the way." When I confess this, I'm thinking of Gunner. It's all I can do not to start crying again.

"Uncle Rex?" Macy asks.

"Yes, niece Macy?"

"We thought...I mean, well...mostly I thought—"

"I was a goner?" he asks. We all nod. "I was turned while running and shooting and somewhere along the way everything just went black. Next thing I know I'm in the weeds and these clowns are dragging me to my feet."

"I thought you were shot," I say. "By the drone."

"'Fraid not," he says with a sly grin he turns on the archer.

Oh, Lord.

I clear my throat audibly, disappointed in him for the first time right now. He pretends not to notice.

"There's a few vacancies in our neighborhood, if you want to try to find someplace nearby," Indigo offers, ignoring Rex. "At least there you'll have heat and shelter."

"Hate to break it to you," Rex says, "but that power surge that just broke open the skies—if that's what that was—it means no more drones, but it also means no more heat, no more electricity, no more anything electronic."

Now she's all eyes on him. The concern in her gaze is the first truly identifiable emotion. At least now we know she's human.

"For how long?" she asks.

"Could be awhile," Stanton says, his tone rather ominous. "Months. Years maybe. Possibly even decades depending on the altitude and damage."

"So what does that mean for us?" Indigo asks.

Rex gives her a grim smile, then says, "What my brother-in-law is so eloquently trying to say is, until we hear otherwise, we're pretty much screwed with a capital F."

END OF BOOK 1

SNEAK PEEK OF *THE ZERO HOUR...*

THE ZERO HOUR: CHAPTER 1

Some people are always talking about how when you need someone, *anyone,* that when your friends fail you and your family abandons you and humanity plummets into a mire of its own making,
at least you have God.

But what if you need Him and all He's got for you is closed
lips and a cold shoulder? Well, the answer becomes simple:
you're on your own.

I tell myself it's better this way. But it's a lie. It was a lie when
the world was normal and it's a lie now that it's not. Every so
often, when I think back to the beginning, to just before all this
happened, when I think about all the drama that used to breed,
gestate and grow legs not only in school but between my parents
at home, I think I might actually believe in the high merits of
solitude.

At one point I might have even told myself the apocalypse
would be a welcomed reprieve from real life. That if civilization
fell, I'd no longer feel so alone. Surely the threat of extinction
would bring us all together, not as one social group or another,
but as human beings, right?

I allowed myself the indulgence of these grand, foolish
thoughts because the unthinkable had happened and I suddenly

found myself grappling with a new reality, one with ragged edges and the everyday reminder of my mortality.

The pillars of this once cultured world shuddered and disintegrated. Much to my dismay, to my absolute horror, people didn't turn *to* each other the way I had hoped, rather they turned *on* each other with a sort of sick desperation. Now that I'm up to my teeth in it, my perspective has shifted. I am no longer that naïve girl from before. The world is different, I am different, and nothing is guaranteed, not even the survival of our species.

My name is Indigo, and this is my story.

THE ZERO HOUR: CHAPTER 2

My dad is leaving me, and honestly, it feels like the worst time ever. This day was coming, I knew it was, and I knew it would feel like this, but still...

"I won't be gone long," he says. "Two days for sure, three tops."

I give my father a pair of big empty eyes; I show him my most neutral face. This will be my first time at home all alone and though I'm eighteen—certainly no child—a first is a first.

First my mother, now him.

My mother was a different circumstance though. She fell for some high society pretty boy who pitched her the dream life, and a few months after that, she left me and my father for him. Leaving tore a gigantic hole in our life, one we're still raw over. At least we have each other, though.

But now he's leaving, too. Unlike my mother, however, he's coming back. I wish I weren't so dependent on him, but he's all I have, and even though I'm not very good at telling him this, I'm grateful to have him.

"What am I going to do for the next three days?" I ask.

He shrugs his shoulders and gives me a sheepish grin. He knows I don't really have any friends. He also knows I'm not prone to getting into trouble, so perhaps he's thinking that leaving me here by myself is a no-brainer. Well, it is for him. But it's not for me, not at all. I make the face.

"What?" he asks with a laugh.

"I guess sometimes I just wish Mom were here," I admit, although I know the weight behind this statement is too much to bear right now, for either of us.

His subtle amusement fades.

"Join the crowd, Shooter," he says, gathering up his things— car keys, cell phone, wallet.

My dad calls me Shooter because it sounds better than archer. Mostly I'm into archery, but occasionally I shoot guns, too, therefore, I'm a shooter.

Shooter.

Mom split a few years back. She's gone now, but not all the way gone. Every so often she calls to see how I am, how school is, how life is treating me.

"It's amazing, Mom," I answer, deadpan. "Just amazing."

She once said she loved my dry humor. I'm still not sure if she was being sarcastic, or if she was for real.

Now when she calls, I say, "Hang on, I'll get Dad," to which she says, "You know I'm calling to talk to you."

Of course she is. She doesn't talk to my dad. Even though he's super chill, good looking and usually on his game, she's avoiding him like the plague. Even *I* know she doesn't want to take responsibility for what she's done, for how badly she hurt us.

When she first went and demolished our family for this promising new beau of hers, after a few weeks passed, she called and I asked how things were. To her, everything was fairy dust and rainbows. She was in love. Now two years later, she's doing everything she can to hide the remorse in her voice. It's there, though. I can hear it.

Beneath the reflective surface of those still waters, an under-current of discontent is churning. It's a restless undertow she's desperately trying to hide. Sometimes I think when she's done with Tad (yep, the home wrecker has a name and it's a really dumb one!), I wonder if she'll come crawling back to my dad. Even worse, I wonder if he'll take her back. I hope he doesn't. She doesn't deserve someone like him.

Anyway, I'm no psychologist and I'm not going to pretend I understand anything that has to do with relationships—especially marriage—but even I can see she's not where she needs to be in life. The woman has no clue what she wants. If she hadn't cheated on my dad the way she did, I would almost feel sorry for her.

But she did, so I don't.

So now she lives with Tad a few miles from here, and it still feels too close. I've been to their home half a dozen times and I swear to God, I don't like it. It's too large and too ostentatious and it's really cold inside. Not cold like the weather, or ice cream —rather it feels cold the way you describe something as empty, something devoid of a soul. That brings me to Tad.

Oh, Lord...*Tad.*

I don't like talking about him since he pretty much stole my mom from us, but whatever. He's a small part of my life whether I like it or not. I'd tell you all about the guy, but I don't want to waste too much time subject of Tad because of teenage angst over your mom's new squeeze is just a tad too juvenile and annoying, even for me.

After going to my mom's new place for dinner for the first time, my father asked me how it was. What he was really asking for was intel, gossip, my most judgmental take on what has become enemy territory.

Naturally, I embellished.

"Tad is a bit of a douchebag with a tad more hair gel than a man his age should have. And he's a tad bit condescending when he talks to me, acting like I should be more of a girly girl like mom, and not some practically flat chested tomboy who likes to shoot things and fantasize about driving muscle cars."

The way I said it, honestly, I've never seen my dad squirm like that. Was I being a bit too dramatic? A tad too self-deprecating? Perhaps.

"That kind of language is unbecoming of a woman," my dad said, completely ignoring what I thought was a brilliant play on words.

"Did no one ever tell you? Douchebag isn't a bad word. It's an adjective people like me use so we don't have to say a-hole."

"Whatever," he said, half amused. "And don't say those things about yourself. You're perfect the way you are."

The one thing not lost on me was my dad referring to me as a woman. I'm a senior in high school and ready as ever to get out of the cesspool of bullies and narcissistic cliques and teachers telling me how I should think rather than how to do math or science or where to properly place a dangling participle. I feel like an angsty teenage girl who doesn't quit fit into the world around me. What I don't feel like, however, is a woman.

To me, a woman has a job. She has bills and credit cards and appointments with the salon and maybe even a personal shopper. She has a place of her own, a few different guys wanting to please her, and she has sex. Lots and lots of chat-worthy sex.

So no, I'm not feeling so much like a woman. But if I've got to start somewhere, then staying home by myself for a few days will be the next step in the evolution of yours truly. It'll be like a trial run of growing up. And I'll tell you this...the first thing I'm going to do is *not* get up at six a.m. The second thing I'm planning for is more sleep!

Not that I'll tell my dad any of this.

I won't.

Right now the two of us are standing in the kitchen with a morning chill pressed on our windows and the outside world black and silent. I'm in my pajamas with bed head and sleep crusted eyes not wanting my dad to leave.

"Will you let me know when you get there?" I ask, folding my arms. "Because San Diego is a long ways away."

He's eating toast, skimming his itinerary one last time.

"I will. You have a list on the counter. Alarm code. Emergency credit card. Keys to the gun safe if you need it. Plus there's a hundred dollars in there for food and gas. And you know where all the emergency numbers are, so..."

"Yeah," I whisper.

He glances up at me, gives me a look, then opens his arms and says, "Come here." I go to him, and he pulls me into one of his amazing hugs. I won't lie, I'm a daddy's girl. He lets me go after a minute or two, tells me he loves me then says, "Will you please, please, *please* make sure you go to school?"

"I'm going to give it my best," I say on the tail end of a long yawn, "but I can't make any promises this early in the morning."

He frowns at me, but that's because he knows I love teasing him. And right now I'm only teasing him because I don't want him going away. I don't want him leaving me all alone.

"I got you a little something for when I'm gone," he tells me.

It's not hard to see how much he cares about me, how much he loves to dote on me. It's one of my favorite things about him.

"You did?" I ask, feigning surprise.

"It's in my office, on the desk. I'll call you when the conference lets out tonight, then again before it starts back up in the morning. Keep your cell phone on, okay?"

"Ten-four," I tell him with pouty eyes.

Outside, he fires up his new Dodge Challenger. It's matte black, lowered on beefy custom rims and it's got some pretty cool headlights, specifically the blood orange halo surrounds. With the shaker hood, the hearty rumble of the Hemi engine and glowing reddish-orange eyes, this beast has a life and personality of its own. The minute we saw it, we both fell in love with it, and that's how Dad got his new car. Of course, with him getting a new car, I couldn't help but ask about his old one.

"Sweetheart," he said with the most endearing smile, "my old car is your new car, if you want it."

Hell yeah I wanted it!

Anyway, as my dad is leaving, I wave to him one last time, then stand there in my pj's and listen to the Detroit engine grumbling its way down Dirt Alley. I won't lie, the sound is beyond intoxicating. The second his wheels leave the packed earth and touch asphalt, Dad gets on it and that sexy black beast rips a hole in the early morning silence.

Had I known that was the last time I was going to see him, I would have hugged him a tad bit harder and a tad bit longer.

YOUR VOICE MATTERS...

Emerging authors always get that writer's high reading great reviews from readers like yourself, but there's more to a review than an author's personal gratification. As independent writers, we don't always have the financial might of New York's Big 5 publishing firms, and we'd never shell out a bazillion dollars to Barnes & Noble for that ultra-prime shelf space (*yet!*).

What we *do* have, however, is far more valuable than shelf space or movie contracts or all the marketing money in the world: we have you, *the devoted reader.*

If you enjoyed this series, I'd be immensely grateful if you could leave a quick and easy review (*it can be as long or as short as you want*). To leave a review, just visit *The Last War* product page on Amazon.com (where you bought the book). Simply scroll down to the review section of the main page and click or tap, WRITE A CUSTOMER REVIEW, and voilà, you're in!

Not only do reviews like yours help this series get the exposure it needs to grow and thrive, reading your kind reviews has become the highlight of my day, so please be sure to let me know what you loved most about this book. Please note, the way Amazon's review system works is five stars is good, four stars is alright, and three stars or less are just degrees of no bueno.

*If you happen to see any errors (typos, etc...), they sometimes show up uninvited and can get overlooked (sad face!), feel free to shoot me a quick email at contact@ryanschow.com. Thank you!

Made in the USA
San Bernardino, CA
17 July 2019